The Devil Wears Baccarat 3

Jatoria C.

The Devil Wears Baccarat 3

Copyright © 2024 by Jatoria C.

All rights reserved.

Published in the United States of America.

All rights reserved. No part of this publication may be reproduced, distributed, or transmitted in any form or by any means, including photocopying, recording, or other electronic or mechanical methods, without the prior written permission of the publisher, except in the case of brief quotations embodied in critical reviews and certain other noncommercial uses permitted by copyright law. For permission requests, please contact: www.colehartsignature.com

This is a work of fiction. Names, characters, places, and incidents either are the products of the author's imagination or are used fictitiously. Any resemblance of actual persons, living or dead, businesses, companies, events, or locales is entirely coincidental. The publisher does not have any control and does not assume any responsibility for author or third-party websites or their content.

The unauthorized reproduction or distribution of this copyrighted work is a crime punishable by law. No part of the book may be scanned, uploaded to or downloaded from file sharing sites, or distributed in any other way via the Internet or any other means, electronic, or print, without the publisher's permission. Criminal copyright infringement, including infringement without monetary gain, is investigated by the FBI and is punishable by up to five years in federal prison and a fine of $250,000 (www.fbi.gov/ipr/).

This book is licensed for your personal enjoyment only. Thank you for respecting the author's work.

Published by Cole Hart Signature, LLC.

Mailing List

To stay up to date on new releases, plus get information on contests, sneak peeks, and more,

Go To The Website Below...

www.colehartsignature.com

Note to Readers:

First, I want to say thank you for supporting me. I am beyond grateful. Next, Roman's book is the final book in this series. I know Kofi's book is highly requested, but he will have his own story in the future. Last, this book is a DARK romance. I know must of my readers are used to my antics and are prepared for a wild ride. With that being said, here are some trigger warnings to be aware of, graphic violence, profanity, explicit sexual scenes, torture, mental illness, and injuries involving fire.

Buckle up and enjoy.

I want the kind of love that ignites a burning need inside. I want the kind of love that sets my soul on fire- Jatoria C.

Previously...
ARI

Four Months Later

Submit. I had an assignment due at midnight, but today was going to be a long day, so I got up early and got it done. If a black woman doesn't do anything else, we are going to get us some degrees. I was currently taking online classes for my master's in nursing. When I graduate, my husband will buy me my own practice as a graduation gift.

I had more than enough money in the bank to purchase my own small practice, but my husband would lose his shit. I turned my computer off and stood up to leave my office. My office, as I called it, was really just the bedroom next door to our bedroom. I had everything taken out and redecorated with all the tools I needed to help me graduate in a year and a half.

When I walked into our bedroom, my reflection in the mirror caught my eye. My stomach was flat for the first few months of my pregnancy, and then one day, I just woke up with a baby belly. The bigger my stomach grew, the more reality sunk in that I really was about to be someone's mother. Today, I turned twenty weeks, and we would learn the gender at my doctor's appointment later.

Where in the hell is my husband?

My thoughts drifted to Constatin, and I smiled. Our marriage had blossomed so much over the last four months. After he found out about my pregnancy, he started getting psychiatric help from a woman who was nothing short of heaven-sent. A lot of her clients were criminals, which is why she was in such high demand. From what I heard, her estranged father was in the mafia. That is why she decided to help the people who had backgrounds tied to criminal organizations, but who knew if that was really true?

Her methods could sometimes be unorthodox, and they varied depending on the client. In Constatin's case, she focused heavily on healing his childhood trauma. He was born with such a great deal of pressure on his shoulders that he didn't allow himself to be a normal child like other kids did.

"Ari!" Constatin yelled my name from downstairs.

Speaking of the devil.

"Here I come!" I yelled back before giving myself one more glance in the mirror. Then, I picked up my purse and walked down the stairs. To my surprise, my husband wasn't standing at the bottom of the stairs as he usually would be. The only person I saw was Emet standing outside the kitchen.

I told him he acts like he is the pregnant one because all he does is eat!

"Baby," I called out to him when I entered the kitchen. He was talking to two people with his back turned to me.

Hmmm... my husband wasn't big on handling his other business in the house.

Confused, I got closer and then stopped.

Is that my mommy?

My mommy gave me a smile but continued talking to my husband and the man standing in front of him. The man was tall; he and Constatin were almost the same height, and he had a bald head.

Who the hell is he? And why is everyone acting like I'm not the most important person in the room?

"HELLO!" I yelled.

"I told you she got a temper. I do not know why you insist on calling her your baby girl," I heard my husband say to the man and laugh. Before I could cuss his ass out for talking about me to strangers, he turned around and moved to the side.

Oh, my God! Please, God. Don't let this be some kind of trick.

Staring back at me was the man who always protected me, the one who saved my life, my own personal superhero.

I burst out crying like a big ass toddler.

"I told you she was going to do that, too. Our baby has her emotions all over the place," Constatin tried to whisper to my daddy, but I heard him.

One minute, my daddy and I were just staring at each other, and the next, I was in his arms. I hadn't felt my daddy's arms around me in over ten years, and the child inside me didn't want him to let go. Small arms wrapped around the other side of me. I knew my momma's touch from anywhere. All three of us embraced each other until my mother stepped away.

"We can hug some more later. Right now, I want to know what my first grand baby is."

My father and I laughed, but he eventually stepped back. My handsome husband was standing there patiently, letting me have my moment.

"How did you do this?" I asked him.

"For you, there isn't anything I wouldn't do. The day you told me what happened, I had Kofi pull his files, and the rest is history. He's a free man, and his murder charge has been dropped from his record."

Mentally, I made a note to give Kofi a big kiss on his cheeks. He was always working hard for our family.

My husband reached out to grab my hand and led me out of the kitchen. My parents followed us. Mikey had bought himself a new Ford Excursion when he found out I was pregnant.

He and Emet had been arguing over who would be the baby's godfather, and my name was 'Bennet,' and I wasn't in it. That was a decision between my husband and them. My husband opened the door for me and helped me into the car, and then did the same for my parents.

The doctor's office parking lot was empty when we pulled into it. My psychotic husband didn't like to wait to have his child checked on, so he would pay for the doctor's office to be closed during my appointment times.

Mikey parked his Excursion and then got out to open the doors for everyone. Emet pulled in behind us and parked beside Mikey. We had to wait for Emmett to go inside the doctor's office and check each room. When Emmett came out and told us everything was clear, we entered the waiting area and were immediately taken to ultrasound.

The ultrasound tech helped me climb onto the exam table and told me to lift my shirt. My hands shook as I did what she asked. She opened the lip of a cool white tub of gel and applied the clear blue liquid over my entire stomach before placing the ultrasound wand on it. We all looked up at the ultrasound monitor to see that the baby was curled up, sucking his or her thumb.

"Are you guys excited to find out what you're having?" the ultrasound lady asked.

"Excited is an understatement," I replied. In all honesty, it didn't matter to me if I was having a boy or a girl. I promised to protect my child and love him/her with every inch of my heart, regardless of what gender I have.

The lady moved the ultrasound wand around my stomach a few more times before pressing down in one spot. She squinted and smiled.

"Congratulations! It looks like y'all are having a boy!"

My husband, who had been quiet the entire time, was now cheering like his favorite football team had just won the Superbowl.

My father reached over and gave him a hug. I couldn't wait to hear the details behind my father's release because he and my husband were too comfortable with each other to have just met personally.

The ultrasound tech spent a couple more minutes taking pictures of the baby before she used a paper towel to wipe the cool gel off my stomach. She helped me back down off the exam table, and we were escorted into the doctor's main office.

We didn't stay inside her office for long. She measured my belly and then told me everything looked fine and to come back next month. My husband was trying to convince me to have a natural birth like his mother did. But I politely told him that he can kiss my entire natural, black ass.

Speaking of his mother, when we got back inside the Excursion, that's where we headed. The relationship between her and me continued to grow after everything that happened since the night I popped up on her doorstep.

Today, she was cooking me a big feast to celebrate learning the gender of her grandbaby. I was so happy that she was getting the chance to meet my parents. I believed they would all get along nicely.

When we pulled into his mother's driveway, Roman, Alexander, and Kenya were already there. As soon as we walked through the door, my best friend and her small baby bump were waiting. Kenya and I agreed that every time one of us got pregnant, the other would, too. That way, all our kids will be close in age and become best friends, like her and I.

She wouldn't find out what she was having until next month, but I was hosting her gender reveal party. Kenya led me to the dining room, where everyone was. When I walked inside, everybody cheered. There were balloons hanging and baby decorations everywhere.

In that moment, my heart had never felt so full. I glanced around the room at all the people I had grown to love and felt immensely blessed. My love story was an unconventional one. It was not one with softness and light. No, my love story was one full of darkness and pain, And I would do it all over again in a heartbeat.

ROMAN

I leaned back in the corner and watched my family as they celebrated the future birth of my nephew. Mom had gone all out, cooking and baking a lot of traditional Romanian and American dishes. I wish my father were still alive. He would have been so happy to learn that Constatin was having a boy. Some of his reasoning would have been unethical, but nonetheless, it would have made him happy. Out of the corner of my eye, I watched as my older brother approached me.

Hmmmm... he looks serious.

He stood in front of me and stared at me. I kept my expression blank and waited for him to tell me whatever brought him into my personal space.

"I know you have been running around here, killing people and setting their bodies on fire. And before you try to deny it, I followed you yesterday and watched you kill a person with your bare hands and set them on fire. Now, last time I checked, the mafia did not have any current problems that needed to be resolved. That worries me.

"Tonight, I decided to be your big brother when I approached you instead of your Nasu. As your big brother, I feel like I was not there for you when Father passed like I should have been. This is me making it up to you. Constatin reached into his pocket, pulled out a black card, and handed it to me. On the card were the words, "Brittany Gabriele. Psychiatrist," and nothing else.

Was he sending me to a psychiatrist? What the fuck!

"In my heart, I am hoping that you are killing as a result of PTSD and not because you just want to be a serial killer.

We all kill people, stupid.

"Your first appointment is scheduled for Monday at 9:00 PM. Roman, you will attend these appointments every week, and you will continue to attend until she feels like you're healed. Now, that is a direct order from your *Nasu*." Constatin reached his arms out and tried to hug me. I just stared at him until he dropped his arms and walked away.

I stayed in the same corner for another ten minutes until the itch became unbearable. Without saying a word to anybody but my mother, I left. My home was only twenty minutes away. I only had two security guards who watched my home, and they were not allowed to be anywhere near the front door. Their only job was to protect the perimeter.

My father used to make me always walk around with two security guards until I kept killing them. After I killed the six or seventh one, he made up an excuse to my brothers about me not needing them anymore because I had my brothers to protect me, and they believed him. I parked my car in my driveway and got out.

The itch was getting stronger. It was taking everything in me to walk calmly to my front door, unlock it, and enter. When I got in the house, I immediately walked to the back and down the stairs to my basement. Before I got to the bottom step, I could hear chains rattling.

"You miss me?" I asked Tom or what was left of him. Tom could not respond because he did not have his tongue or any more teeth left in his mouth. "You missed one hell of a satisfying meal. I know how you love my mother's cooking. I am so full; I feel like I could burst."

Tom made incomprehensible noises before crying. He had not eaten anything in four days, and I knew he was starving. I walked over to my tray and picked up a scalpel before advancing toward him.

"Enough of the small talk. It's time to play," I said, grinning.

Brittany

"Shit. Damn, baby," my boss moaned while I threw my ass back, pushing his dick as deep inside my pussy as it would go.

Greg was a blessed man. His dick was long and thick, and I could feel every inch of it as he rammed it inside me from the back.

Do I want a salad or salmon and broccoli for dinner? Hmmm, I have to go over the file I made for my new patient. I might as well order salmon and broccoli.

"Fuck, Brit. I love you, girl. Shit. Tell me this pussy belongs to me," Greg pleaded.

His thrusts were starting to get jerky, and I knew it wouldn't be long before his nut filled up the condom he had on.

Hell naw, this pussy is the property of Brittany Gabriele. Let me moan so we can hurry this up. I despise being uninformed when it's time to meet a new client.

"Ahhhhhh, it feels so good. Nut in this good ass pussy," I purred.

It was a good thing my head was down in the bed, or he would have caught the way I rolled my eyes. The sound of my round ass clapping as he fucked me got louder. Greg tightened the grip he had on my hips and began to gasp.

One second, two seconds, three seconds, four seconds, five seconds, six seconds.

"Brittanyyyyyyyy!" he screamed my name before slumping his sweaty ass body over on my back.

Finally. Ughhhhhhhh. We had been fucking for almost fifteen minutes, and I was ready for it to end fifteen minutes ago.

"That was fun. Can you lean up? I need to go take my shower. Please lock my door on your way out. I will see you bright and early in the morning," I stated as I lifted my head off the bed.

The pressure lifted off my back, but he was still holding my hips tight.

"Why do you always do this? Seriously, what am I doing wrong? You only let me fuck you once a month. Every time I try to have a serious discussion about where our relationship is heading, you shut the discussion down. Damn, I haven't even flushed the condom down the toilet, and you are already putting me out," Greg whined.

Men who whine are so unattractive.

My head turned around, and I gave his naked body a quick glance up and down before briefly looking into his light blue eyes. Gregory Hilton was a handsome white man. He was six feet tall; his body was lean and fit, and he had an innocent face that made it hard to tell his real age. It was obvious from his salt and pepper colored hair that he was an older man, but most people wouldn't guess he was fifty-six years old.

I was one of eight psychiatrists who worked in his psychiatric clinic downtown and have been there for three years. He and I had been fucking for two out of the three of those years. That's the longest any of my arrangements have lasted, but it was something about the way he begged that intrigued me enough to keep dragging this situation on.

"Nothing has changed, and I am tired of having this same discussion. You knew before you came over here that it's just sex.

Can you please let my hips go and leave? Go enjoy the rest of your night."

"You would rather be a whore instead of settling down and letting me love you the way you deserve," he mumbled.

"Now you know better than to resort to such vulgar language when describing me. Use your big boy words."

"As a repercussion, from what I would presume was a traumatic relationship or upbringing, you have a fearful avoidant attachment style and narcissistic tendencies."

My lips lifted slightly upward in an almost smile. His diagnosis of me was right in some ways and wrong in others.

"Good job. Now, it's up to you if you want to continue having our monthly rendezvous, but our time is up for today."

Greg mumbled something else under his breath, but he said it too low for me to hear him. He pulled his flaccid dick out of me and snatched the condom off before reaching down to pull his black pants back up. Quickly, he zipped his pants and stormed off to my bathroom. Fifteen seconds later, I heard my toilet flush and the bathroom water running.

"Goodnight," I told him when he came out of the bathroom a minute later and finished putting back on the rest of his clothes.

He didn't reply, but I didn't expect him to. He missed a few buttons on his shirt, but I didn't say anything. Finally, he turned around, walked to my bedroom door and out of it, leaving me alone like I preferred.

Men were so predictable, especially men of a certain status. They all believed that money and sex could make any woman weak in the knees for them. I was not like most women, though. Emotions such as love and empathy weren't things I could feel. Phoebe, my cat, was the only thing in this world that I had any kind of feelings toward. The only reason I even entertained men was that it fed my ego.

When I finally gave in to Greg's advances, I made it clear what to expect, and he agreed to the terms. Instead of sticking to the agreement, he tried to change the terms, which has resulted in him becoming disappointed and throwing small temper tantrums. No matter how many times I told him I didn't want anything serious, he kept trying as if I would eventually change my mind. He couldn't fathom the idea that I would turn down the chance to be Mrs. Hilton. He even promised to make me a partner in the clinic if I married him. What he failed to realize was that there was nothing he could do or say to make me love him. I was just not capable and had no desire to pretend.

I waited until I heard my front door open and close before I climbed off the top of my crimson-colored bedroom set. My bedroom was simple and tidy. I had a gold dresser set that matched my gold nightstand. My bed set and a small rug that lay in front of my bed was crimson red. The only picture on the wall was the picture right above the top of my bed. It was a photo I took five years ago for my twenty-fifth birthday. In the picture, I was naked with a thick ivory-colored sheet wrapped around my thick body.

Hastily, I glanced at the picture before turning away from it and walking into my cream and gold-colored bathroom. For the next forty-five minutes, I showered and did my nightly hygiene routine. Afterward, I put on my tan colored silk pajama set and my tan bonnet to protect the wrap I had done on my hair in the bathroom. The only thing left for me to do was remove the top cover off my bed before I exited my bedroom.

My house was a three-bedroom located in a decent part of downtown Atlanta. I wasn't far from the restaurants and shops downtown. Compared to most of the people I associated with, my house was small. It was only me living here, and I didn't need a lot of space. One of the empty rooms, I turned into a guest bedroom and the other an office, even though I rarely used the office.

I descended the stairs, headed down into the kitchen, and then walked into my laundry room. My laundry room was attached to my kitchen. Inside the laundry room, I put the top cover inside the washer and started the wash cycle. When I finished, I exited my laundry room and walked over to my normal seat at my dining table. On the dining table were my phone and a couple of files I had put there right before Greg came.

"Wasn't my phone turned face down?"

A dry chuckle escaped my mouth, and I shook my head. Greg wasn't down there long enough to go through my phone. He probably picked it up and thought about looking through it before deciding against it and putting it back down. My phone didn't have a lock code on it. If he wanted to hurt his own feelings, he could have. For every action, there is a reaction. I scrolled through my contacts until I found the number for a local restaurant only about twenty minutes away in Buckhead. They had the best honey-glazed salmon. It only took me a couple of minutes to place my order for delivery.

While I waited, I picked up the beige folder and looked at the name I had written on the side. Roman Bucur was the sibling of a current client. His brother was one of my easier cases, and besides the fact that he ran the Romanian mafia, I considered him more rational than my other clients. His wife, Ari, was also nice, and we occasionally texted each other. I flipped the folder open, ready to study all the data I collected on his brother, Roman, and paused.

Inside all my clients' files, I always clip a small picture to the top of it. My eyes scanned the picture of the unsmiling face and cold mahogany-colored eyes. A shiver ran through my body, causing me to frown. Roman was a good-looking man, but I had a strict no fraternizing with mafia men policy, thanks to my daddy dearest. My eyes slowly left his picture, and began to read the notes I had gathered. By the time the food arrived, I felt more prepared for my first meeting with Roman in the morning. I ate my dinner before cleaning up my kitchen and placing my files back into my brown leather tote bag.

"Phoebe," I called out to my cat.

Phoebe was antisocial and always disappeared when company came over. She was also mean and didn't mind attacking people who got too close to her without her consent. The cabinet door under my sink made a squeaking noise as it opened. I shook my head as I watched phoebe climb out of one of her favorite hiding spots before approaching me. Phoebe was a Bombay cat with all-black fur and a mixture of gold and green eyes.

"Hey, Sour Patch," I greeted her by my nickname for her before squatting down to scoop her up and carry her up the stairs.

When we got back inside my bedroom, she jumped out of my bed and sauntered over to her cat bed. She snuggled inside it and grabbed her favorite kitten ball to play with. Phoebe didn't shed a lot of hair, but I still liked to use a lent brush to quickly wipe myself down before climbing into my bed. Sleep found me easily that night as I rested peacefully.

Roman

I glanced down at my Patek Phillipe Skelton Dial watch to look at the time. My first counseling session with the psychiatrist was two hours away, and I only had a small amount of time to play before I had to leave my home to drive to the psychiatric clinic forty-five minutes away.

This shit is going to be a waste of time, and I hate wasting my time.

The feeling of irritation flooded my body as I walked down the stairs in my basement. The feeling did not last long. It disappeared as soon as I reached the bottom step and looked over at Tom. Yesterday, I took two big buckets full of soapy cold water and dashed his body with them to help with the egregious scent drifting from his body. It did not do much, but it was intriguing to watch him trying to scream and then shake from the cold temperature of the water. He was only allowed a few slices of bread and bottled water every three or four days. The lack of food and water was not only a form of punishment, but it kept him from defecating all over himself and the basement floor. He was placed directly over the drain I had installed inside my floor when I first purchased my home. Every time he peed or I beat him bloody, it would flow down into the drain, making less of a mess. Tom slowly lifted his head to look at me before a few tears dropped from his eyes. He had so many bruises and cuts all over his body that it looked like he had been beaten by multiple people. His body was not going to last much longer, and I had been doing everything in my power to prolong his final moment.

"Unfortunately, I don't have a lot of time today to play," I told him as I approached the metal tray that held all my tools. I picked up a scalpel and the blow torch before walking over to where I had him chained to the floor. On his neck was a collar with a loop on it. Through the loop was a chain that led from his neck to the ceiling. Tom's hands were chained behind his back. The chain was connected to the basement floor, giving him only enough room to stand and lie down. He opened and closed his mouth, but nothing came out of it. When I severed his tongue, I had to use the blow torch to cauterize the small piece left to keep him from bleeding to death or choking on his own blood.

"Get up," I demanded and waited patiently for him to gather his strength to stand up.

"What part of your body should I cut off today?" I asked him while looking him up and down.

I used the scalpel and cut him a few times across the top of his chest and then watched as the blood dripped down his naked body. It was amusing to watch, but I did not cut him deep enough for the wound to leak blood for long.

"Arm or leg?"

Good suggestion. I think I should stab you in the leg, too. We played with your arm yesterday.

Tom's legs were not chained down. The first day I kidnapped him, he was belligerent when he woke up. He kicked the hell out of me when I approached him, but he paid for it when I took a bat to his ribs. After that day, he hasn't lifted his filthy feet to put them on my body again. I walked closer to him and picked up his left leg before plunging my scalpel into the center of his thigh. Up and down, I removed the scalpel and plunged it back into his thigh several times until I was satisfied with the amount of blood leaking from his thigh.

Now, it's time for my favorite part.

Excitement coursed through my veins, and my dick swelled in my onyx-colored slacks as I moved to put the scalpel back on my tray. Tom's eyes widened a little as I approached him again. He had been down here long enough to know what I was about to do next. I turned the blow torch on and stared into the icy blue flames, momentarily hypnotized. Seconds went by, and I could feel the precum leaking from the top of my dick before I reached back down and used my left hand to stretch Tom's leg back out. With my right hand, I lowered the blow torch and burned Tom's flesh in the same spot where I had just stuck the scalpel in him several times.

The burning scent of human flesh had me biting down hard on my bottom lip. It didn't take long for his wound to stop bleeding profusely. I turned the blow torch off and walked swiftly over to my metal tray to set it down. The walk back over to Tom was a stiff one, and I was relived when I stood back in front of him. My hands moved in sync to unbutton my pants, unzip my zipper, and pull my dick out of my briefs.

"Fuck," I groaned as I squeezed my dick hard.

Spit flew out my mouth and onto my dick. My hands were already slightly lubricated with blood. Up and down, my right hand went jacking. My eyes rolled to the back of my head, and I groaned again at the feeling of ecstasy building inside me. I jacked my dick for a few minutes before pausing and then aimed my dick toward the wound on Tom's thigh. Nut shot out of me and onto the new stab wound. Slowly, my heart rate decreased, and my body went back into a relaxed state. My dick and briefs were sticky, and I shook my head, upset with myself for the lack of control I exhibited.

My eyes went back to the watch I had on my wrist before I reached down to pull my pants back up. It took me twenty minutes to clean my scalpel and the blow torch before stripping and burning the suit I had on. Before I left my basement, I checked to make sure Tom's chains were still tight.

"That was fun, Tom. We have to do it again soon," I said as I walked up the basement stairs.

I made sure the basement door was closed and locked before I walked to my stairs and up them. My house had six bedrooms and seven bathrooms. My room was the first one on the right. I entered my bedroom and walked into my closet to grab another onyx-colored suit. Thirty minutes later, I was dressed and heading out of my front door. I hit the key fob to unlock my canary yellow Bugatti Chiron super sport 300 and climbed inside. As soon as I pulled out of my driveway, I hit the gas, speeding to make it to my appointment on time.

Brittany

Not only was Mr. Roman Bucur ten minutes late, but he strolled into my office without speaking a word. That was ten minutes ago, and nothing had changed. He sat across from me in one of the two ivory-colored lounge chairs I had for my clients. I didn't do group sessions, and I only took married couples on rare occasions. Females were a hit or miss with me. Some of them liked me, but most of them didn't. Their feelings toward me weren't important to me, but I tried to avoid uncomfortable situations in my workplace as much as possible.

"Mr. Bucur, your brother set this appointment up and was adamant about your participation."

Interesting. I was under the impression that he would want to please his big brother. It was clear he didn't give a fuck about pleasing anybody.

Roman didn't even blink his eyes. He was staring off into space as if I wasn't even there, but I knew it was an act. He was paying attention to everything happening. This was the eighth question I had asked him that he ignored. There was a reason I was highly requested, and that was because I knew how to draw my clients in regardless of whether they wanted me to or not.

I stood and walked over to my desk. On top of my desk was a

candle I lit five minutes before his appointment time. The candle was seasonal and spread the aroma of a mixture of pumpkin, cinnamon, and vanilla around my office. It was one of the smaller candles that wouldn't take more than a couple of hours to burn. Under it was a small platter. The candle had burned enough that the platter already had dried candle wax on it. I picked the candle up and carried it to the glass end table next to my ivory chair before sitting down. Roman turned his head slightly and stared at the candle, watching the flames dance.

Hmmm, Roman is a pyromaniac. After he killed all his victims, he set them on fire. I wonder if it was because it was an easy way to dispose of the bodies, but it was more than that. Roman's eyes had been cold and uninterested the whole time he was here, but now I see interest swirling in the middle of them.

While Roman stared at the flames, I scribbled in my notebook what I observed before placing the pen back inside and closing my notebook.

"Would you like to burn me with the candle wax?"

Roman blinked before frowning. He moved his head back toward me and gave me a quick glance up and down.

"Is that a trick question?" he replied. His voice was deep and raspy, surprising me. For Roman to be the youngest, his thick beard and deep voice were intriguing.

In the picture I got of him, I knew he was a handsome man, but now that I had the chance to see him in person, the word handsome wasn't a strong enough description. From what I could tell, he was covered in tattoos. His face was lightly tan colored, and he had high cheekbones. His black beard and mustache surrounded plump, pale pink lips. Now that his dark mahogany-colored eyes appeared less cold, they were more attractive. He cleared his throat, and I blinked.

"No, it is not a trick question. I am a straightforward kind of person. If you agree to answer three questions for me, and the answers are honest and in-depth, you may use this candle beside me to burn my flesh anywhere but my adult body parts."

Silence filled the room again. Roman turned his head away from me and back toward the candle before he nodded his head in agreement.

"Mr. Bucur, I believe that was confirmation, but I need direct communication."

Roman turned his face back toward me and stared into my eyes. For some reason, I felt the skin on my arms warm up, but I remained still.

"My brother may know me a little more than I expected. Nonetheless, Ms. Gabriele, I agree to the terms as long as I get to burn you first before I answer the questions."

He smirked while he responded, and I had the urge to smile. Of course, I didn't give into the urge. He was testing me. He didn't believe I would really let him burn me.

"I agree."

Roman stood and straightened his suit jacket before approaching me. The cologne he wore was the same one his brother wore. It smelled expensive, manly, and sweet. A strange combination, but together, it created a potent scent. Roman reached down in front of me and picked up the candle. It was impossible for me to miss the bulge forming inside his pants.

Mentally, I made a note to write down that fire turned him on sexually. It wasn't uncommon. Murder itself was known to be an aphrodisiac, but in Roman's case, murder wouldn't be enough to arouse him. He needed fire to turn him on. After Roman picked up the candle, he surprised me by walking behind me. Curiosity almost made me turn around to see what he was doing, but I didn't because that's what he wanted me to do.

"Good girl. Lean your head a little to the left for me."

His deep voice sent shivers through my body, and I felt my pussy walls clench. Sex wasn't something that normally excited me. It was more of a tool I used to control people whenever I saw fit. My head leaned to the side, and I stared at my plain white walls. The first touch of the hot candle wax on the side of my neck caused me to briefly close my eyes. Pain wasn't something I feared, and the sting I felt from the candle wax melting into my skin didn't faze me. What did faze me was when Roman leaned down and blew on the spot where he burned me.

You cannot fuck this man. He is in the mafia. Plus, men like him don't understand I am not available for more than sex.

I heard his clothes move slightly as he stood back up.

"You are not a good girl. You are as naughty as they come. You may have the world fooled, but I know when someone is wearing a mask. Am I the crazy one, Brittany Gabriele, or are you?"

What the fuck? Nobody has ever been able to see through my mask. From the age of six, I have studied humans and their reactions to perfect masking.

The next drop of candle wax was lower on my neck, causing some of the wax to flow down my blouse.

"Now, I am jealous. The candle wax got to feel your beautiful breast before I did."

My lips mushed together. I refused to respond to him. Roman was attempting to use sexual statements to get into my mind, but I had used the same tactic too many times to fall victim. I expected to feel his breath on my neck, blowing at the new spot, but instead, the candle wax was poured onto my neck at the same spot. The feel of his lips against the lower part of my neck was unexpected. Roman kissed the burn mark before whispering in my ear.

"Now, you have my attention, but is that a good thing, Doctor?"

He kissed my left ear before walking back around the front of me. His dick print was no longer a bulge but had grown to full mass and was lying on his right leg.

Impressive. It has been a while since I saw a dick that big.

After he placed the candle back on my nightstand, he blew it out and then turned to have a seat in the same chair. Most people would have gotten up and used the bathroom to clean the hardened candle wax off, but his appointment time was ending soon.

"Your brother mentioned that your family refers to you as the mystery. How do you feel about that?"

Roman leaned back into the chair and crossed his leg before answering.

"I honestly do not care what people label me. If anything, I can understand why they would feel that way, but I am how I am. When I find something or someone intriguing, I have no issue paying attention or communicating. If I am not interested, I will not pretend like I am."

Manipulative and enjoys going against society norms.

"Let us talk a little about your crimes. Did you plan your kills out, or were they random acts?"

Roman's eyes darkened, and he gave me an intense look.

"Are you the feds?" he asked. His voice was no longer welcoming but had turned frigid.

"No. All my clientele are people from the underworld. Mostly mafia members and people with a history of dangerous felonies. My lips are sealed, and anything said will remain confidential. My life depends on it."

"How do I know you are not lying?"

"You don't, and I won't provide any of my clients' names to prove that I speak the truth. I do speak the truth, though; I don't care enough about anybody to lie."

Why did I add the last part? It's the truth, but he didn't need to know that.

He was silent for a moment before I watched his body relax again.

"My kills are random in some ways and not random in others. The people I kill are not random, but when I kill them is. Whenever I get the urge, I normally react."

He owns a kill list but acts on his impulsiveness to kill.

"Our time is ending. My last question for this session is do you have deep emotions for any person in your life?"

Roman smiled at me, and it was genuine. His teeth were so white, I would bet money that he got them bleached regularly.

"Are you flirting with me, Mrs. Bucur? If you are asking if I have a woman in my life, the answer is no. Well, I did not have one before I laid eyes on you."

Charming bastard.

"The question was not one of a flirtatious nature because I do not sleep around with men in the mafia. Can you answer the question, Mr. Bucur?"

Roman's eyes squinted, and I could tell he didn't like my response. That was a personal problem. It took him a few seconds before he answered.

"Yes, my brothers mean the world to me. My mother is my heart, and I will kill you over any one of my extended family members."

He speaks the truth. Hmmmmm.

"That concludes today's appointment time. Please try to be on time next Monday. The secretary will hand you a card with the new appointment time on your way out," I replied, dismissing him.

Shock covered his face, but he did as I asked, stood up, and walked out of my office. After Roman closed my office door, I opened my notebook and picked my pen back up to make my final notes. During our session, he showed signs of antisocial behavior, lack of remorse for his victims, the desire to go against society norms, and impulsiveness. What Roman suffered from was not curable, but it could be manageable. He had a severe case of antisocial personality disorder with psychopathic tendencies. In layman's terms, he was a psychopath.

My diagnosis wasn't surprising because he was born the son of a cold-hearted, ruthless ruler of the Romanian mafia. There is a reason why nature vs. nurture is so widely discussed among psychiatrists or anybody in a related field. Psychopaths are born psychopaths due to a chemical imbalance in the brain that can be credited to genetics. Sociopaths, which is what I am, are not born sociopaths but are made sociopaths typically from their upbringing or a traumatic experience.

Roman

For the first time in the last six weeks, I had no desire to torture Tom. It had been two days since I stabbed him in his thigh, and instead of hurting him as soon as I got home from work, I showered and climbed into my bed to get some rest. Today was no different. Instead of leaving work at five in the afternoon, I stayed until seven to finish a current marketing plan. Now, I stood in my kitchen, tearing bread into small pieces and adding them to the plate of mashed potatoes I had just made for Tom. He could only swallow food after no longer being able to chew. For some unknown reason, I decided to give him more to eat tonight.

When I finished making his plate, I walked out of my kitchen and down the hallway until I reached the end of it, where my basement was located. I slid my hand inside my pants, pulled the key out to unlock the door, and then walked inside. After closing the door, I descended the stairs.

I wonder if Brittany likes jewelry. She did not have any on during our first session.

Ms. Brittany Gabriele had been a constant presence in my mind. No matter how hard I tried, I just could not stop thinking about her. Every time I closed my eyes, all I could see was her milk chocolate skin. The way her cold almond shaped amber colored eyes peered at me as if she could see through my soul. Brittany was different from any other woman I had ever dated in multiple ways. The women of my past were rich and bland. Just something to stick my dick in, but none that I would ever claim as my own.

Brittany was a lot of things, but bland was not one of them. She had the perfect round face, a Nubian-shaped nose, and plump milk chocolate lips that, as of two days ago, belonged to me and only me, even if she did not know it yet. During our session, she had remained seated in her chair, but there was no way to hide how her thick thighs and ass fit against the navy-blue skirt she wore to work. I was honest with her when I told her I was jealous that the candle wax got to touch her perky C cup sized breasts before me.

Brittany was chocolate, curvy, and crazier in the head than me. We were a match made in heaven, but something told me we would have to go through hell before Brittany would see it that way. An image of Brittany dancing in a ring of fire appeared in my mind. Damn, my future was hot, and I was prepared for the burn. Our next appointment was four days away, but I planned to see her before then. When I reached the bottom step of my basement, I paused to clear my mind before I stepped down.

Tom was lying on the floor, his body curled into a ball, when I reached the bottom of the stairs. His arms were stretched out, relaxed on each side of his body. Normally, he would have his arms crossed and wrapped around his shoulders tight to provide some kind of heat and comfort to himself. The basement had two vents in the ceiling that allowed air or heat to circulate in the room if I had the system in use. The temperature in Atlanta was in the low sixties today when I woke up, prompting me to turn the heat on. I had not used the system in the previous weeks because the temperature in the house was around seventy, so I did not require it.

I walked further inside the basement and laid his plate of food right in front of his face.

"You have five minutes," I said while Tom stared at his plate.

He closed his eyes, and I watched as he inhaled deeply before opening his eyes back. Tom used his right hand to push the plate as close to his face as he could get it before lifting his head and lowering it onto the plate. He used his lips to suck the food into his mouth and swallow it. It took him two minutes to eat everything on his plate. When he finished, he dropped his head back onto the basement floor and sighed. I walked back over to pick up the plate and left the basement without saying anything else. A few minutes later, I tossed the plate into the trash and washed my hands. My cellphone dinged and then vibrated inside my pants pocket.

Kofi must have finished the background check on Brittany.

Quickly, I pulled my cellphone out of my pocket and was disappointed when I saw the name on my screen.

Kenya: Come let me out of this damn room!

Alexandur must have put her in time-out again.

Me: Why? Where is my brother?

Kenya: Because if you don't, I will call your mother to do it and then tell her when she gets here how you refused to come help me. Your brother dumb ass is gone to get my food!

Kenya had always been feisty, but now that she was pregnant, her mood swings were driving my brother crazy. I will not hear the end of it if she calls my mother. Alexandur will just have to be mad.

Me: I will be there in fifteen minutes.

My phone dinged again when I slid it inside my pocket, but I ignored it. Instead, I walked out of the kitchen and to my front door to leave. I took the keys out of my pocket and hit the unlock button on the key fob to unlock my car door. A couple minutes later, I pulled out of my driveway. It was late, after eight in the afternoon, and traffic was light. I made it to Alexandur's house in ten minutes. I pulled into the driveway and parked next to Kenya's car.

We all had the keys to each other's houses. Briefly, I wondered why she did not call Kofi, but knowing him, he was busy with Constatin training or gathering intel on his computer. I put Alexandur's house key into the lock and unlocked the door before entering his house alarm code. We all lived in mansions, but my mansion was the smallest because it didn't include extra rooms such as a theater or wine cellar. None of that stuff interested me. As I walked up Alexandur's stairs, I wondered how I would get inside his bedroom. He was the only one with the key. When I approached his bedroom door, the only solution I could come up with was to kick the doorknob off, and that's what I did. It took me several kicks before I kicked the doorknob through the door and into Alexandur's bedroom.

"Finally!" Kenya stated. She stood up from the couch she was sitting on and wobbled over to me. Kenya was almost seven months pregnant, and her stomach was bigger than before every time I saw her.

"What did you do?"

"I threatened to leave him because he brought home my food, and the order was wrong. He told me he wouldn't go fix my order if I didn't get off my feet because they had been swollen the last few days. My dumb ass listened, and as soon as I closed the door, I heard the lock. I swear if I didn't love your brother so much, I would kill his ass."

I shook my head before turning around and walking away.

"Bye, brother," Kenya yelled when I reached the stairs, but I did not respond.

I was ready to get back home, shower, and go to bed. On the way out the door, my cell phone dinged again. I pulled it out when I reached my car to see who it was and smiled. Kofi had sent me Brittany's background check. That night, I lay in my king-sized bed and memorized sentence after sentence in the report Kofi sent over.

The next morning, I woke up a couple of hours early and rushed to get ready for work. On my way to Bucur International Wine Corporation, I stopped in a nice neighborhood not too far from downtown. I parked my car two houses down from Brittany's three-bedroom brick house and waited patiently. I sat in my car for almost fifteen minutes before Brittany exited her house, walked toward her 2021 Bolton grey series 5 BWM, and got inside. She had a little over thirty minutes to get to work and did not waste time pulling out of her driveway.

A few more minutes passed before I started my car and drove two houses down. I parked in the same spot that Brittany had just pulled out of and cut my car off. When I stepped outside, I kept my head high and did a quick scan of the surrounding houses. I took calm steps toward Brittany's front door as if I had been there a dozen times before. Everybody in Brittany's neighborhood was middle-aged, diligent people, and the few people I did see outside were rushing out of their homes to their cars. Brittany was not the kind of person who made small talk with her neighbors, but I still worked quickly with my lock pin to open her front door and enter her home. Once I entered, I closed her door and was greeted by her cat.

"Hey, Phoebe." I squatted to greet her.

Phoebe stared at me for a few moments before slowly approaching me.

"Good girl." I petted her softly when she was within arm's reach before standing back up to find Brittany's kitchen.

In the hallway, I took mental notes of the few pictures she had on the walls and the way everything was neat and tidy. Everything was in neutral colors, and she had no family pictures up. In the kitchen, I opened her refrigerator and freezer to see what kind of foods she liked to eat before doing the same to her kitchen cabinets. Brittany was mine, and it was important for me to learn every detail about her.

After I walked out of her kitchen, I ran up her stairs and opened each door in the hallway until I found her bedroom. In her bedroom, I looked through the clothes in her closet and dresser drawer. I smelled a few items to memorize the scent she used to wash her clothes. I was careful not to move any items too much out of place, and I only stole one pair of her cotton panties. Lastly, I walked into her bathroom and used my cellphone to take pictures of her personal items before walking back out.

Time was moving by steadily, and I had spent almost twenty minutes inside Brittany's home. It was time for me to go. On my way to work, I could not fight the smile that appeared on my face. Brittany had become obsesia mea (my obsession), and she did not even know it. I laughed maniacally.

Brittany

Maybe: Roman Bucur: Good morning, obsesia mea (my obsession). I miss you. I have been counting the seconds, minutes, and hours until I see your beautiful face again. What do you want to eat for lunch? I have already covered your tab for the rest of the year at your favorite restaurant downtown. All you have to do is call and place your order, and it will be delivered at the time of your choosing. The boss has been informed to notify me if you do not order any food for the day, and I will personally choose your meal and deliver it. The only exception is on the weekend because soon you will be spending those days with me, and we will choose our meals together. I know you are about to leave for work. If my brother gives you any problems today, just let me know. Have a great day, obsesia mea (my obsession), and remember that you belong to me.

I was heading out my front door for work when my phone vibrated inside my purse. In a rush, I dug inside my purse to retrieve it. Roman was unpredictable. I should have expected him to ignore the warning I gave him in my office on Monday. Roman Bucur had crossed my mind every day at the most random times. Today was Friday, and we wouldn't meet again until Monday morning. He was right, though; I did have a session today with his brother Constatin.

Me: Mr. Bucur, my personal number is on the business card for emergencies ONLY. Is there something wrong that I should be aware of? Are you having thoughts of harming yourself or someone else?

Roman should be taking a few medicines every day, but his brother made it clear that he did not want me to prescribe him anything. It was not an uncommon request. The majority of my clients wanted me to "fix" them without taking the medicine they needed.

Roman: I am a bad man, baby. I am always thinking about harming someone. No, I have no desire to hurt myself. Why would I want to harm myself when I just met you, the woman I will marry one day?

I wonder if this kind of behavior is normal. Does he also have obsessive-compulsive disorder?

Me: How often do you feel like you have met a woman or man that you believe will one day become the person you will marry?

Roman: You are so clever, but I hate to disappoint you. Before I walked into your office, I had no desire to beg in a relationship or get married. You are special obesia mea (my obsession).

Just when I thought my life had become too monotonous, I get tempted by a handsome devil in a suit that I would have enjoyed toying with. Any other time, I wouldn't mind having fun, but Roman went against the rules. I never break my own rules.

Me: Have a good day, Mr. Bucur, and please only message me if you are having an emergency. This is unprofessional and will not be tolerated.

Roman: Brittany, I know everything there is to know about you. Please do not insult my intelligence. You do not follow professional standards. Nonetheless, I must take a trip this weekend with my other brother Alexandur. Behave, baby, while I am away.

This motherfucker is delusional.

Instead of replying, I slid my phone back into my purse and then walked out of my front door. For the last few days, I had gotten a weird, prickly feeling every morning when I walked to my car. I looked around my neighborhood before I reached to open the car door. Nothing stood out, but I couldn't help but feel like I was being watched.

You are tripping, girl. Get your ass in the car and take your ass to work.

I climbed into my BMW and closed the car door. After adjusting the music to my liking, I pulled out of my driveway and drove to work.

As soon as I made it inside my office, I powered my computer on. Next, I removed my plaid red and black overcoat and hung it and my purse up on the wall hanger. I sat at my desk to pull up the notes for the five clients I had coming in today when someone knocked on my door. All psychiatrists in this clinic reported to work an hour before any clients were scheduled, which let me know it had to be someone who worked here knocking.

Whoever it is knows I am in here; they better twist the knob for entry or stand out there looking like a fool.

There were a few more knocks before my office door opened. Greg walked through with a bouquet of flowers in his hand.

"Brittany, what new guy you got sending you roses?" His voice was laced with an attitude as if he had the right to question me.

"Thank you for bringing the bouquet in for me. If you need me for anything business-related, please give me a call on my office phone," I replied, and then I gestured with my right hand for him to place the flowers on my desk.

Greg frowned before doing as I asked. He then proceeded to stare at me while I ignored his presence until he abruptly turned around and stormed out. Our situation was coming to an end. He was getting too deeply involved for my liking.

    I waited a few minutes before I reached out to pick up the bouquet of roses and inhaled their aroma. Receiving flowers wasn't something new for me, but this was my first time ever seeing any blue-colored roses. I picked up one of the stems and placed it on top of my desk before setting the bouquet back down. There was a small envelope attached, and I was surprised to see the envelope hadn't been tampered with. I wouldn't put it past Greg to have opened it before he brought them to me.

    The rarest roses for my rarest gem, the note said. It was signed with the initials RB. There was only one person I knew with those initials, and I was starting to regret letting him pour candle wax on my skin.

    I hope this situation doesn't turn deadly in the end.

    The single blue rose I picked out stayed on my desk while I worked. The day passed swiftly, and lunch time arrived. In my tote bag were some roasted potatoes and fried chicken I had made the night before, but I hesitated to pull them out.

    What are the chances that if I don't place a lunch order, Roman will really show up at my job?

    Seconds went by while I pondered the question in my mind. I liked playing with fire more than most people, but some fires weren't worth the burn. After a few minutes, I picked my phone up and placed a damn order for lunch to be delivered. When the phone call ended, I hit the hang-up button and then pressed number one.

    "Hey, I ordered you some lunch as a token of appreciation for the arduous work you do. It will be arriving shortly," I told my secretary before hanging up my office phone and then getting up and pulling my cold lunch out of my tote bag.

    For some reason, I didn't want to leave the office and go to the break room to warm my food. Instead, I took the top of the food container and ate my food cold. It was very tasty. Lunch ended shortly after, and I got back to work. At a little before three, my last client of the day arrived. Constatin Bucur entered my office. He walked slowly over to have a seat in the chair. His small limp gave off a dangerous vibe that could be felt in the air. I waited a few seconds for him to get comfortable before I sat up a little in my chair and opened my notebook.

"Good afternoon. How are you feeling today?" I asked him.

"Happy. My wife's stomach is growing bigger every day with my son. My empire has been running smoothly. There have not been any new enemies lurking around, begging for me to end their pathetic little lives. The wine company is projecting an annual increase of three billion. Alexandur finds out what he and Kenya are having next week. Kenya and Ari have decided to throw this extravagant baby shower together. She told me to tell you to expect an invitation. Oh, and Roman called me Monday night to inform me that he is going to marry you. I have no complaints at the moment."

Constatin did not smile or smirk as he answered my question in depth. He was like me, a straightforward person.

"Have you had any thoughts of self-harming?"

"None. Nothing will separate me from my wife. She is my world."

Constatin knew death was uncontrollable, but I decided not to point it out. Falling in love with his wife gave him a new outlook on life. Love is a powerful emotion, but it was an emotion I hadn't felt in a long time. People believed sociopaths were incapable of having emotions, but that wasn't true. Some sociopaths do experience love. They just feel it in a different way. When a sociopath falls in love, it is in a deep, obsessive-possessive way. Feelings such as empathy or guilt are what sociopaths do not feel. Every person walking this earth is different in some way, no matter what they look like or what kind of medical diagnosis they have. In my case, I do not believe I am capable of loving anymore. That part inside me died when I was a child.

"Did you do one activity from the list I gave you?"

"Yes. Over the weekend, I wrote a letter to my younger self

and told him that perfection was impossible. I am the CEO of an international multibillion-dollar company, I am the Nasu of the Romanian mafia, and I am human and allowed to make mistakes without punishing myself."

The Constatin sitting in front of me was different from the man who first sat in front of me a few months ago. He was a frigid man with the world on his shoulders. Now, he spoke freely and was learning to love himself unconditionally without adding requirements to it.

"How did you feel after you finished writing the letter?"

"Relived. Before, my mind was stuck in a dark fog, but now I wake up every morning and choose what mood I want to be in."

"That's good. Is there anything you want to discuss with me?"

"Yes. When you and Roman get married, I want to be the best man, not Alexandur."

Damn. I thought if I ignored his statement about his brother, he would let it go.

"Marriage is not something I desire, nor is a relationship."

Constatin smiled at me before laughing. I didn't see anything funny.

"I told you during one of our meetings how my father gave me and my brothers a nickname when we were younger. I am the mind, Alexandur is the monster, and Roman is the mystery. Roman is the kind of person you never know what he is thinking, and if he decides to do something, he will accomplish it without failing. My brother has chosen you as his wife, Brittany, and he will not stop until you two are married. "

Statements like that are why I am selective with the rich men I entertain. Rich men who had a lot of power did not like it when they were denied the things they wanted. Doctors, Politicians, and Criminal bosses all have the same mindset. They are narcissistic and competitive as fuck. The majority of them married the woman who looked good on their arm and not the one they loved.

"That's our time for today. Please continue to pick off an activity from the list I provided to you. You are doing great with healing your childhood traumas. Soon, you will no longer need these sessions as often."

Constatin nodded and stood up to leave.

"Welcome to the family," he said on the way out of my office.

Family, my ass. My family was murdered in front of me, and it was because of their own actions.

Roman

It was time for the monthly shipment of cocaine to set sea. Alexandur and I flew into New York early yesterday morning and waited for our ship to bring in our package. The ship was a little late because of the weather. When the ship docked, we unloaded everything ourselves and checked to make sure there were 2400 kilos of pure cocaine on board. Constatin and Alexandur ran into a minor problem with our supplier in Colombia, but Alexandur beat the problem out of him. It was a little after midnight when we repacked another one of our ships with cases of wine that had kilos hidden under them.

Early this Sunday morning, the crew returned to the port and got ready to sail out again. That ship left the port an hour and a half ago, sailing to Peru. Now, my brother and I were on Constatin's private jet on the way back to Atlanta. We had about thirty minutes left before we landed. I had not spoken much during the flight. My mind was on Brittany. Constatin told me about their session Friday. She was determined not to give us a chance. My pride kept me from reaching out to her this weekend. Now that the weekend was ending and I was on my way back home, those two days confirmed what I already felt inside. There was no amount of space or time away from Brittany that could make me not think about her. Brittany was created from above and sent to Earth to be my wife.

"Brother, we all have bets on how long it is going to take for you and Brittany to get married. I bet three months. You will make sure I win, right?"

Alexandur interrupted my thoughts about obsesia mea (my obsession) for a foolish question. I turned my head away from the window to glance over at my big brother.

"No."

"If you do not, I will inform Constatin that you are the one who kidnapped Tom."

What the fuck! How does he know about Tom?

I turned my head back toward the window without replying.

"I can tell you are wondering how I found out, even if you are acting like you do not care. You were the one who left the information for Kofi. Kofi would only protect someone close to him, and that only left a few suspects. The day we went after Elizabeth, you had left work early. The pieces were not hard to follow when you know your little brother is sneaky. Is he dead?"

"What do you win?" I asked.

"Constatin will name his son after me."

"The answer is no. If the baby cannot carry my name, he will not carry yours."

I did not have to look at my brother to know my answer pissed him off. All my life, I have studied both of my brothers. Alexandur's threat was an empty one. He would not tell on me.

The rest of the ride was a silent one. Alexandur was probably trying to figure out how to win their silly bet, but Constatin would not name his son after either of us. Constatin was raised to protect us at all costs. When we were younger, Alexandur and I would run around playing while Constatin stood back and watched over us. I do not question my brother's love for us, but I also knew we were made to be a burden to him. He will not name his child after anyone. Instead, he will give his son his own identity because he was never given the chance to have an identity.

When I made it home, I showered and changed into my night clothes. Alexandur and I had eaten a few slices of New York-style pizza before we got on the plane. I was still full and decided to spend an hour or so having fun with Tom before I went to bed. As soon as I opened the basement door, the smell of death greeted me. Quickly, I descended the steps to see if Tom had died. He lay on the concrete floor with his eyes closed.

"Tom," I called out, but he did not move.

I approached him and then squatted to check his pulse. He had a pulse, but it was weak.

Decisions. Decision. Decisions

I stood and walked over to the metal tray that held all my tools. Instead of picking up a tool, I slid my hand inside my pocket and pulled my cellphone out. I scrolled my contacts until I saw Obsesia Mea (my obsession) and hit dial. The phone rang four times before she answered.

Brittany: Roman, why are you calling me so late at night? Do you need to reschedule our visit in the morning?

Roman: Of course not. I am eager to see you. I miss you. You told me to call if I had thoughts of harming myself or someone else, and that is what I am doing.

She did not speak, but I could hear her sitting up in the bed.

Brittany: Talk to me, Roman. Tell me if the thoughts are about you or someone else.

Roman: It is about the man I have chained to my basement floor. His body is fading, and I am ready to end his life. Torturing him no longer excites me.

Brittany: Why are you calling me and telling me this? How long have you been torturing him?

Roman: You told me you would not tell the police, and I believe you. Even if you did, I know my brother told you he suspects me of killing those two officers who tried to arrest my sister-in-law. I did kill them. If you did decide to tell on me, there would just be more dead police officers in Atlanta. The answer to your second question is for too long. I have been torturing him for over a month.

Brittany: Kill him. I don't see the point in prolonging the inevitable.

I picked the hammer up off the tray and walked back over to Tom. Using only my left hand, I smashed the hammer into Tom's head. After the first hit, Tom opened his eyes and tried to move, but after I smashed him in the head a few more times, his body stopped moving. His eyes were still open, but there was no life in them. Blood and brain matter had flown all over the bottom of my pants and the concrete floor. I lifted the hammer and hit him two more times in the head before dropping it. Brittany was still on the phone. She had not made a sound, but I knew she was still listening.

Me: He is dead.

Brittany: Okay. I will see you in the morning for our appointment.

Me: Wait. I want to discuss my feelings while I watch his body burn.

Brittany inhaled and exhaled deeply, clearly aggravated with me, but she did not hang up the phone. She really was a rare gem. Brittany did not care about me killing, but she took her job seriously enough that she would remain on the phone to let me express myself. How intriguing. I walked over to the table where my metal tray was, picked up the can of gasoline, and walked back to Tom. The whole can of gasoline was poured on top of his dead body before I walked back to the table and set the gasoline back down. Next, I grabbed the lighter. If I had not been on the phone, Tom would have been set on fire, but I was not ready to end the conversation.

Me: I am going to use the clothes I have on to set his body on fire and get rid of evidence. It will only take a moment.

Again, she said nothing. I put the phone on the table and rushed over to Tom's body. Quickly, I stripped down to only my briefs. All my clothes were tossed on top of Tom's dead body except my shirt. I used the lighter to set it on fire and then tossed it with the rest of the clothes. My dick immediately got hard. My long legs took big steps to walk back to the table and pick the phone up. The call was still going. Inside, my heart sped up, and I felt all warm and gushy.

Me: Baby, his body is on fire, and my dick is begging for a release. I would give billions to have you here with me. Your chocolate, curvaceous body under me on your knees and your mouth wide open. Fuck, the fire burning and your mouth open wide, ready to suck my dick, would be the gift of a lifetime.

Flashes of Brittany's face crossed my mind, causing me to groan loudly. My left hand went into my briefs and pulled my dick out.

Brittany: Bye.

She hung up the phone, but I could hear the need in her voice. Brittany could fight all she wanted, but she was turned on by me. I removed my hand from my dick and put it inside my mouth to get it wet. My legs spread farther apart before I placed my hand back on my dick and began to jack it up and down. My eyes closed, and I pictured Brittany's soft hands moving up and down on my dick instead of my own.

"Yes, baby," I moaned.

Nut shot out the tip of my dick and onto the burning flames. My heart was beating so fast it felt like it would burst through my chest. Nothing had ever turned me on so much. It took me a few minutes to regain my composure before I pulled my briefs off and tossed them on top of the fire. Tom's body took an hour to burn completely, and I watched every second of it.

Brittany

Last night, after I ended the call, I slid my hand inside my panties and masturbated. In my mind, I kept telling myself that I couldn't control who I had chemistry with. You can have strong chemistry with a person and not be compatible with them. Plus, when my alarm went off on my phone this morning to wake me up, I felt more relaxed and refreshed than I had in weeks. In the shower, I took my time washing and exfoliating my body before getting out to finish the rest of my routine. On most workdays, I would do a light beat or go bare-faced, but today, I did a full beat on my face. Now, I stood in front of my dresser, looking in the mirror at myself.

Girl, your parents might not have done a lot of things right, but the one thing they did was create a beautiful child.

I decided to put on another one of my high-waisted skirts today. This one was blue, the same color as the blue roses Roman got me. Under the high-waisted skirt was a pair of black leggings. I topped the look off with a black blouse that swooped down into a v-cut that gave a sneak peek of my breasts.

You are playing with fire. Don't cry when yo' dumb ass gets burned.

I gave myself one more glance over in the mirror, ignoring the voice in my head, before picking up my black tote and leaving my bedroom. Today, I would enjoy lunch on Roman, so I walked past my kitchen and out my front door. That prickly feeling returned, but I was running behind and did not have time to waste looking for a figment of my imagination. When I made it to work, I parked and swiftly got out of my car. By the time I entered the clinic, I was a little over ten minutes late.

"Good morning, Brittany, I was just asking your secretary if you had called. It's not like you to be late," Greg said.

He was talking to me, but his eyes were roaming my body. The secretary was watching him stare at me like a hawk.

"Good morning," I muttered to them both before rushing past them to walk into my office.

Sooner rather than later, I would have to officially end this situation with Greg. When I first agreed to mess around with him, he promised that when we decided to end this, it wouldn't affect my job. If he let his emotions change his mind, then I would begin job searching immediately. I had no strong emotional ties to this clinic, but I was comfortable with the patients I had. Routines were important to me. The first thing I did was power on my computer, and then I hung up my jacket and purse. I sat at my desk and then frowned. Someone was knocking on my office door.

I guess now is the best time.

Greg entered my office and had a seat in the chair in front of my desk.

"How can I help you?" I asked.

"Are you fucking your clients?"

No, he didn't. If men did not have anything, they had fucking audacity

"No. I currently have no sexual or romantic ties to anybody I have a professional relationship with."

Bitch ass.

Greg leaned forward a little and squinted as if that would make the words I said to him clearer.

"Are you including our relationship in that statement?"

"Greg, we never had a relationship. We fucked around once a month. That is it. Nonetheless, I believe it would be best for both of us if we maintained a strictly professional relationship moving forward."

Greg's pale face turned red, and he abruptly stood up. If he thought standing over me was intimidating, he was incorrect. In order to be intimidated, I had to be in fear of someone. A dry chuckle escaped my mouth before I could stop it.

"You think it's funny playing with my heart?"

Omg. Nobody told you to get your heart involved in the first place.

"No, I have no thoughts at all about your heart or the emotions you feel in it. I have a client coming in shortly, and I need to study the notes I took in our last session. Leave, Greg. Now is not the time or place for this."

"Let's get something straight. This is my fucking office. YOU work for me. It will do you a hell of a lot of good to remember that," he threatened. I didn't reply. He turned around and stormed out of my office, slamming the office door behind him. If the secretary hadn't been suspicious before, she definitely would be now.

After Greg left my office, I leaned my head back in my chair to contemplate. Everything was rapidly changing in my life, and I didn't like it. Ending the situation with Greg wasn't important by itself, but when you add in Roman coming into my life like a wrecking ball, I felt like my control was slipping. My alarm went off, reminding me that my first appointment would be arriving soon. I opened the right desk drawer and pulled a lighter to light the candle on my desk. A few minutes later, there were a couple knocks on my office door before Roman entered.

What the hell kind of cologne is that? Whatever it is, it smelled too damn good.

Roman entered my office in an all-black Tom ford suit with a blue tie the same color as my damn skirt. His wearing a suit wasn't surprising. He had one on during our first session. Constatin told me his brother was over the marketing department at Bucur Wine International, a company founded by their grandfather. He also owned a twenty percent stake in the entire company. Their middle brother, Alexandur, owned twenty percent, too. Constatin owned forty percent, and the last twenty percent was owned by their mother. I was rich, but they were wealthy.

"Good morning, baby," his crazy ass greeted me before having a seat.

"Mr. Bucur, that is very unprofessional. Please address me as either Ms. Gabriele or Brittany."

"No," he replied. He smiled brightly at me before relaxing his body into the chair.

Arrogant son of a bitch.

"Last night, you called me while committing a murder. Can you tell me why you felt the need to take a person's life?"

Silence. Roman didn't open his mouth to respond. Manipulation wasn't uncommon for psychopaths. His silence was expected. He wanted to burn my flesh like I let him do in our first session. For now, I would play his game, but in the end, our sessions would not involve candle wax. I stood up from my chair and walked back to my desk with the candle. I set the candle on the end table before sitting back in my chair. Roman glanced at the candle but turned his gaze back upon me.

"Last night, you called me while committing a murder. Can you tell me why you felt the need to take a person's life?" I repeated the question.

Silence.

"Mr. Bucur, if I let you burn me three times, will you answer five questions in return?"

"No, but if you wear this item I brought you, I will answer all the questions you ask in our sessions freely moving forward."

This time, I was the silent one. His request caught me off guard. My eyes zoomed to his empty hands, and I frowned.

Roman caught the action. He slid his right hand into his pants pockets and pulled out a black ring box.

What the fuck? Is this some weird ass marriage proposal?

"Mr. Bucur, I have to warn you, if you are planning to propose a marriage between the two of us, unfortunately, I will have to decline."

Unfortunately, my ass.

"When I propose to you, Brittany, I will leave no room for doubt," he replied.

Roman stood and walked over to where I sat. He opened the ring box and removed the ring before sliding the empty black ring box into his pocket. Roman reached down with his left hand to pick up my left hand and hold it in his arm.

In what world is this not giving a marriage proposal? I swear, if this man drops down to one knee, I am going to kick him upside his head. Maybe that would knock some sense into him.

"Last week, it only took a few moments in your presence for me to realize you were the one for me. I know that sounds insane, but I speak the truth. The next day, I went ring shopping."

Roman stopped talking to slide the damn ring he was holding in his right hand onto my marriage finger on my left hand. The ring was beautiful. It was a pear-shaped blue diamond on a gold wedding band with small diamonds all around the band. The ring had to have been at least three carats and cost millions.

"The ring on your finger is not a marriage ring but a promise. Brittany, I promise to do everything in my power to show you that I am the one for you, just like you are the one for me. I pledge my love, loyalty, and, in our near future, my last name to you and only you. I promise to take care of you and spoil you daily because you deserve only the best of the best. I will protect you, I will provide for you, and I will give your body pleasure until you are weak and beg for me to stop. The only promise I ask from you in return is for you to refrain from removing the ring. When the time comes, I will remove it and replace it with a better ring."

Girl, don't you sell your soul to the devil.

I opened my mouth to decline his offer, but I couldn't stop staring at how beautiful the ring looked. Men had lavished me with expensive gifts before, so how was this any different? Roman reached down to gently grab my chin and lift my face until we were staring into each other's eyes. His brown eyes had an intense glare in them, showing me how serious he was. A feeling of possessiveness spread through my body.

Maybe claiming him as mine wouldn't be so bad. No. What the fuck am I thinking? Not only is he in the mafia, but he would one day want something I am not capable of giving him.

"Roman, the ring is beautiful, but you should know that I don't process emotions the same way other people do. Love is not an emotion of which I am capable of feeling."

"I accept you as you are."

Roman let my face go and turned around to walk back to his seat. He sat back down and relaxed his body into the chair. Silence filled my office once again.

Time is winding down. Do I keep the damn ring or give it back to him?

I glanced down at the ring before looking over at the clock on the wall. There were only ten minutes left in our appointment, and I hadn't done my job. My hands joined together before I placed them in my lap.

"Mr. Bucur, you called me while committing a murder. Can you tell me why you felt the need to take a person's life?"

"The person I killed was responsible for my father's death, and he shot my brother in the leg," he replied.

Revenge was the motive.

"Are all your killings revenge-motivated?"

"No, I kill when I get annoyed as well. My first kill was two security guards my father had assigned to me. They followed me around everywhere, even when I asked them for privacy. One day, I told them my father wanted me to meet them in the woods to practice shooting targets. It was not an unusual request. They drove me to the woods and followed me. When I felt like I was deep enough in the woods, I pulled my gun out from underneath my shirt, turned around, and let off shots. They were caught off guard and did not have time to pull their own weapons before death greeted them."

"How old were you when that happened?"

"Fifteen."

Constatin was worried that his brother would lose his temper and kill someone at the wrong time or in the wrong place. He didn't want Roman to get in some trouble that would be difficult for them to get him out of.

I opened my notebook and scribbled notes inside it. Roman needed a way to ground himself when he felt his temper slipping.

"Have you ever tried mediating?" I asked.

"No, but I will if you do it with me."

"Your assignment this week is to sit alone, close your eyes, and take regular breaths in and out for five minutes. I don't want you to focus on your thoughts. Let your thoughts come and go as they please. Instead, I want you to focus on the noise around you. Listen closely to your surroundings."

"If I am mediating in silence, what is there to hear?"

"You won't know until you try. Mediation is a great tool to train the brain to remain calm and think rationally before reacting."

Roman was quiet while he processed my request before nodding his head in agreement.

"That's our time for today. I will see you next Monday at the same time," I told him while writing more notes in my notebook.

"Bye, baby. Do not forget to order your lunch, or I will be back," he replied. Roman stood and walked confidently out of my office.

I waited until I heard the door close before I stopped writing and closed my notebook back. The sparkle from the ring caught my eye. Roman would have to cut this ring off my finger if he thought he would get it back.

Roman

When I made it back to the office, I immediately started working on the marketing plan for the announcement of the exclusive wine deal we had with Bellagio. My father was a smart businessman, but he was stuck in his ways when it came to expanding and marketing. He preferred to meet with owners of hotels and restaurants to make deals face-to-face. It was a good method, but times have changed. The only social media presence our company had was a website.

After my father passed, I hired a social media manager to expand the company's presence over the internet. The company sales have already expanded significantly. For the announcement of the new exclusive line, I was working on a vision board for a commercial. It will be the first commercial the company has produced. When my grandfather started this company, it was easier to build a successful business and remain unknown because social media was not around. Now, it is almost unheard of.

As a capo in the Romanian mafia, I did not have any social media profiles, nor did I attend certain events for a huge number of well-known celebrities or influencers. That will never change. The company, though, will take more initiative in the limelight. Starting with this commercial. I had even created a small list of celebrities I wanted the social media manager to reach out to. One of them would end up starring in the commercial, bringing even more visibility to the company.

During lunch time, I placed a call to the local restaurant Brittany liked to eat from to confirm she ordered her food. They confirmed, and I ended the call to place an order to have my lunch delivered. When the food arrived, I ate my meal and thought about the session I had earlier that day. The blue diamond promise ring I gave Brittany was rare, just like the blue roses I had delivered to her job last Friday. She did not voice how she felt about the ring, but she didn't have to. It was clear from the way she kept staring at it that she loved it. It was time for me to become more aggressive in my pursuit.

I picked up my phone and sent Kofi a text message telling him I needed to see him. Ten minutes passed before Kofi knocked on my office door two times and then entered my office. Kofi was no longer the nerd he was when I met him. He stood in front of me in a customized black suit, an AP watch on his wrist, and Cartier glasses on his face in place of the large frame glasses he used to wear. He was growing a beard and mustache that made him look older than his actual age.

"What's up?" he greeted me as he took a seat in the office chair in front of my desk.

"I need a favor."

Kofi squinted at me before shaking his head from left to right.

"Every time one of y'all fall in love, I get caught in the middle of some bullshit. If you are about to be torturing innocent bodyguards or cutting on yourself, count me out. Y'all be tripping."

Kofi told me that my brothers and I be "tripping" often. I had to ask Kenya what he meant. She said it is urban Ebonics, which means me and my brothers be doing crazy things. If that is the case, we do be "tripping," as he said.

"You owe me. It is because of you that Alexandur attempted to threaten me into marrying Brittany in exactly three months for a silly bet. He claims he figured out I had Tom all on his own, but Alexandur is self-centered. If it is not about Kenya or beating up somebody who crossed one of us, he does not pay attention to it.

"How is that my fault?"

Instead of responding, I just stared at Kofi until he threw his hands in the air.

"Fine. I might have asked Alexandur if my suspicions of you made sense."

Which is why you are going to spend the weekend babysitting for me.

"Friday, you and I are going to break into Brittany's home while she's at work."

"See, that's that bullshit I be talking about. Why can't y'all find a nice woman, date her for a year, and then propose like normal people?"

"Waiting to claim the person who is meant for you is not normal. It is actually an act of cowardice. Why would I waste twelve months on the person God or whoever is up there controlling shit made for me? No, Brittany is mine, and I will not wait any longer to make that clear."

BRITTANY

"You look beautiful," Benjamin stated before leaning to place a kiss on my left cheek.

This wasn't our first date, and on every one of them, I made sure I looked drop-dead gorgeous. Tonight, I had on a Maria Lucan Hohan Jolie gown in salsa red. The dress showed a good amount of cleavage and leg. My hair had been flat ironed and flowed down my back. I went with a natural beat on my face but with a salsa red lipstick to match my dress. On my feet were a pair of black Jimmy Choo slender stiletto heels. Benjamin didn't look too bad himself. He was a tall, peanut butter complexion man. His face was free of any blemishes except for a small tattoo on the side of his face. He was dressed nicely in black pants with a silk black button-down shirt.

"Thank you," I replied and stepped out onto my porch.

I turned around to close and lock my front door before turning back around to join hands with Benjamin. He led me to his white Mercedes Benz and opened the passenger side door for me. I climbed into his car and waited for him to get in. He got in, and we pulled out of my driveway.

Benjamin was one of my newer clients. He found out his wife had been sleeping with his best friend and killed them both. The betrayal cut him deep and messed with his self-esteem to the point that he started making mistakes at work. He was the accountant for a local street gang called Slime Kings. They were well known around Atlanta but on a small level compared to some of the other criminal organizations I worked with. Benjamin was under the impression that I liked him but wanted to take things slow. In reality, I was doing what I was hired to do as his therapist, and that was fixing his self-esteem issues so he could focus.

"I made us a reservation at La Cuisine."

"Great. I have been dying to eat there for a while, but the reservations are hard to get," I replied.

Benjamin gave me a cocky smile, and I pretended to smile back. The fastest way to boost his self-esteem was to boost his ego, which was why I let him take me out once a month to an expensive ass restaurant and dressed up like a model. This was our third date, and it would probably be the last. He was no longer the nervous, stuttering man he was on our first date.

The rest of the drive to the restaurant was silent and lasted about twenty minutes. Benjamin pulled up to the valet and got out of the car. He walked around to the passenger side to open the door for me and waited for me to get out of the car before joining our hands together. The valet reached his hand out for the keys. Benjamin handed him a hundred-dollar bill and his car keys before leading me into the restaurant.

The hostess asked him for his name, and he gave it. She looked inside a book to locate his name before smiling and telling us to follow her. I could feel eyes watching us as we walked. I knew Benjamin could sense them, too, because he had that cocky-ass smile on his face. A few women even openly stared at him in a flirtatious manner as if I wasn't there with him.

They lucky I wasn't with Roman, or I would have slapped those smiles right off their faces.

It had been four days since I last saw Roman. He had been texting me sporadically since then, but I had barely been responding. The hostess led us to a table near the center of the restaurant.

She waited while we took our seats before informing us that our server would be with us shortly.

"How has work been going?" Benjamin asked.

Before I could reply, my phone vibrated inside my clutch.

"It's been going well. Hold on one second. Let me make sure this isn't one of my clients," I replied. I opened my clutch and pulled my phone out.

Speaking of the devil

Roman: What is the best way to get rid of competition?

Me: What? What are you talking about? I am busy. Is there some kind of emergency?

Roman: Incorrect. The best way to get rid of competition is by elimination.

This man is truly crazy. Why the hell is he messaging me about some damn competition at this time of night?

Without responding, I slid my phone back inside my clutch.

"Sorry about that. I have a new client with heavy psychopathic tendencies. Have things been improving with your job?"

"Yeah. I have not messed up any numbers in a while. If anything, I am working better than I was before I was backstabbed by that bitch."

I nodded without responding. Benjamin was allowed to express himself however he saw fit, but that didn't mean I was going to encourage him to talk bad about his ex. For all I knew, she had a valid reason to cheat on him with his best friend. If she did, then who was I to judge her? He did her wrong, and she returned the gesture. For every action, there is a reaction.

"Good evening. What can I get you two to drink?" the server asked.

"She will be drinking water. Same for me," a deep, raspy voice replied.

The server and I both turned to the right to see if the person attached to the voice was talking to her. My eyes connected with cold, dark, mahogany-colored eyes.

Security, I need help because a bitch is being stalked.

Roman's insane ass smiled at me before sitting right in the seat beside me.

"Who are you?" Benjamin asked him.

"Actually, can you give me and my wife a few minutes to talk to her friend?" he asked the server.

"Who the hell is your wife?" I asked.

The server looked at us both before glancing down at my hand. I didn't even have to look down to see that she had spotted that damn promise ring on my finger.

"Sure," she replied before turning around and rushing away.

If there weren't so many people around us, I would have picked up the knife off the table and stabbed Roman in the side of his helium-filled head.

"Roman, what the hell are you doing here?" I asked. The smell of the damn cologne drifted to my nose, making me even angrier.

Control your temper. Do not stab that damn man.

"Baby, I am here to eliminate the competition," that fool replied.

Now, that text message he sent made sense, but how in the hell did he know I was on a date?

"Benjamin Porter. The son of Kelly and Robert Porter. The siblings of Keisha, Bruce, and Robert Jr. You have a measly thirty-eight thousand dollars in your checking account and another thousand dollars in your savings account. You recently went through a nasty divorce, and the wife took the house and rental property, but she was nice enough not to demand spousal support. Tell me, Benjamin, what did you do wrong today?"

Benjamin's eyes widened, and he stared at me.

"Eyes on me, Benjamin. I would hate to have to ruin these nice people's dinner, but I will slice your fucking throat if you look at my wife again. Now, please answer my question?"

"I don't even know who the fuck you are," Benjamin replied. He stuttered while speaking, and I felt like all the progress I had made with him was gone.

"Benjamin, thank you for a nice dinner. I apologize for my client. He is clinically insane. Please call the office to make a new appointment," I said to Benjamin. I stood to leave, but Roman's voice stopped me.

"If you leave, he will not make it out of this restaurant alive. You haven't had dinner, and you know how I feel about you not eating obsesia mea (my obsession).

I rolled my eyes before looking down to see how serious this fool was. Benjamin dying wasn't a concern of mine, but Benjamin dying in my presence would have Greg down my throat at work, and that wasn't acceptable. Angrily, I sat back in my chair.

"You have three seconds to get the fuck out of my presence, or I will kill you and your family before midnight," Roman threatened Benjamin.

Benjamin looked at me for help, and I did not know what he expected me to say, so I told him the truth.

"He is not my husband, but he will kill you and your whole family. He would probably get away with it, too."

Benjamin gasped before jumping up and rushing out of the restaurant. I didn't have to look around the restaurant to know there were people watching us curiously. No one at the table raised their voices, but it didn't take a rocket scientist to see that Roman popping up created tension.

"What are you eating?" this fool had the nerve to ask me.

"Roman, one of two things are about to happen. I am either going to order an Uber, or you are going to take me home right the fuck now."

Roman turned to the side to look at me. I opened my clutch and reached inside to pull my phone out.

"Okay, but we have to do another date night since this one was interrupted," he muttered.

Roman stood up and reached out to take my hand. I complied and put my hand in his for appearance's sake. He led me back out of the restaurant to the valet.

"I got y'all coming right up," the valet said before rushing away, laughing."

If I wasn't already attached to my ring, I would have thrown it in the middle of traffic, but no one was touching my damn ring. The valet returned a few minutes later with Roman's yellow Bugatti. Roman tipped the man before opening the passenger side door for me. I climbed into his car and buckled my seatbelt. Roman walked around the car and opened the door to get in. When he sat down, he pulled his phone out and typed a message to someone before cranking his car and driving away.

The whole ride to the house, I remained turned away from him and looked out the window. He didn't try to make small talk with me, but the air wasn't filled with tension. Twenty-five minutes later, he pulled in front of my house. It wasn't lost on me that he knew where I lived without me telling him. Obviously, he liked gathering privileged information on people.

"Your food arrived a few minutes ago. It is on your porch," he said before getting out of his car to open the door for me.

"I don't believe I am the right psychiatrist for you. I will send a list of recommendations to your brother in the morning," I told him when I got out of his car.

"You look beautiful tonight, baby. I apologize for not saying so sooner," he replied before turning away from me and walking back to the driver's side of his car.

Ignoring my statement isn't going to change anything. This situation has gotten out of control.

Roman got in his car and turned his head to watch me through the passenger side window. I turned around and walked to my front porch. On the porch was a brown paper bag with food inside. The aroma of the food drifted out of the bag and into the air when I picked it up, causing my stomach to growl.

Ordering my favorite food isn't going to change anything either, Mr. Bucur.

I unlocked my front door and entered my house without turning back around to look at Roman's crazy ass.

Roman

It was pitch black in the room. I stood in the corner so close to the wall that it was as if I was a part of it. The only movement I made was to lift my wrist and check my watch every few minutes. Time ticked by at a snail's pace until the watch on my wrist finally passed one minute after twelve p.m. A smile crossed my face as I stepped out of the shadows.

Benjamin lay stretched out in his bed, sleeping wildly. I was raised to be a man of my word. It was hard fighting the urge to come straight here after dropping Brittany off, but Benjamin did leave the restaurant as I asked. In return, his life was spared all the way until two minutes ago. Time was up, though, and it was time to wake him up. I approached his bed and pulled my gun from my waist.

"Benjamin, get up," I said before tapping my gun against his head.

He wiggled around a few times before he slightly opened his eyes.

"Hey, you remember me?" I asked.

Benjamin frowned before closing his eyes and opening them again. He opened his mouth to scream, but I slid the gun between his lips and cocked it.

"If you scream, I will blow your brains out," I warned him.

"Please, please," he begged.

"Stop begging me and sit up. I just want to ask you a few questions."

Benjamin began to cry, but he sat up in the bed like I asked him to.

"Have you slept with my wife?" I asked.

"Brittany didn't tell me she was married," he pleaded.

His response made me angry. I lifted my gun and slapped him across the face a few times.

"Have you slept with my wife?"

"No. I promise I haven't. She-she wanted to take things

slowly. We have only been on a few dates; we haven't even kissed," he whimpered while holding the right side of his face.

"If you had stuck your filthy dick inside what belongs to me, I was planning to chop it off. Now that I know you have not, that changes my plan."

He whimpered some more and held his hands up together in a prayer gesture. Death could be so unfortunate at times. Benjamin did not know he was putting his life at risk when he took Brittany out for dinner tonight. Pointing fingers and placing blame was wasted energy, and it would not change the outcome of the night.

I smashed my gun into his face and head several times until he lost consciousness. I had screwed a silencer on the end of it before I broke in. My gun slipped between his lips, and my trigger finger moved on top of the trigger. I pulled the trigger once and watched half his head splatter on his headboard. He was dead, but I pulled the trigger one more time to see how much more blood and brain matter would come out. It wasn't as much as the first time, but now blood and brain matter were all over his sheets and headboard. I slid the gun out of his mouth and put it back into my pants.

His kitchen was the first room on the left when I walked through the front door of his house, and that was where I headed. I opened several cabinets until I found a bottle of olive oil. I untwisted the top on the olive oil and dashed it over the eyes on the stove top before turning all four of them on high. There was a kitchen towel hanging on the wall next to the stove that I grabbed and spread over the top of the stove. The towel caught fire immediately.

Satisfied, I jogged to his back door and slipped back out. I jogged through his backyard and jumped the fence where I had my car parked. Once I made it safely inside my car, I sat and waited. It took ten minutes before I saw the bright orange flames through the living room window. It would not be long before the fire spread throughout the whole house. My hand hit the start button, and I cranked my car up and pulled off.

I drove a few blocks away before turning around and driving back toward Benjamin's house. As I got closer, I heard police and fire truck sirens loudly in the air. I turned down his street, and it was no longer quiet like it had been ten minutes before. There were several police cars parked in front of Benjamin's house, two fire trucks, and neighbors standing in the yard. I kept my face looking straight ahead as I drove past the mayhem. Benjamin's house burned until only the foundation of the house was left untouched by flames. How tragic.

Brittany

"Two bouquets of roses in a row. Am I wrong for feeling jealous?"

Yes, you are.

Greg entered my office holding a new vase of blue roses. Constatin had his session earlier, and I gave him a list of highly qualified psychiatrists that I believed would be a better fit for his brother. He didn't even look at the list; he just slid it into his pocket. For some reason, that irritated me, but I couldn't pinpoint why. This weekend, I booked an appointment for a massage and facial to help ease my mind.

"Brittany," Greg called out. The vase of roses was no longer in his hands, but they were on top of my desk.

I blinked a few times before looking up at him and putting a smile on my face.

"Did you hear what I said about your client, Benjamin Porter?"

Ohh, fuck!

"No, I had zoned out. Can you repeat it?"

"Mr. Porter's house caught on fire. The fire department arrived too late to save him or his house. They believe it was caused by a kitchen fire. The fire started in the kitchen from the stove. The poor guy was probably cooking and fell asleep."

House fire, my ass!

"Yeah. That sounds terrible. I will have my secretary send his family flowers for the funeral arrangement."

Greg nodded but continued to stand in front of my desk.

"Is there anything else I can help you with? I just finished typing my notes into the computer, and I was about to shut down and gather my things to leave."

"I don't want to end our relationship."

If you knew what I knew, you would be running the hell up out of here.

"We have no relationship. You are my boss, and I am your employee. We used to sleep around occasionally, but that has run its course."

I turned my computer off and stood up.

"What are you so afraid of? Am I not good enough for you? I know you like the way I fuck you, and I have enough money to take care of you. I really don't understand it."

"Greg, I can't do this with you today."

It seemed that he liked getting his feelings hurt or something. I moved from my desk to grab my tote and my jacket. He really stood there like a statue and watched me put my jacket on, take my keys out of my tote, and walk around him to leave my office.

When I made it to my car, I opened my tote and pulled my phone out to send a message.

Me: I know what you did. Stay the fuck away from me!

I slid my phone back inside my tote and hit the start button on my car. On the way home, I let the music play, easing some of the tension I felt in my body. By the time I pulled into my driveway, my irritation levels had decreased significantly. On the walk through my driveway, I wondered why Roman didn't respond. Why kill someone for going on a date with me and then ignore when I texted him? I put my house key in the door and opened it. One of the things I liked most about my job was that I was off every weekend. I entered my home and locked the door before walking down my hallway toward my kitchen. Tonight, I would order some food and wine and cuddle up in my bed to read a good book.

"Hey, baby. How was your day?"

I stopped walking and turned to the left to peer into my living room. Roman's psycho ass was sitting on my couch, typing on his phone.

How in the hell did this man get in my house?

"Roman, I am exhausted. I don't have time for you and your foolishness today."

"By the time we land back home on Sunday, you will feel much more relaxed," he replied and stood up.

"Land? Roman, get the fuck out of my house before I call the police!" I yelled.

He walked closer to me but stopped six feet away. Today was my first time seeing him in something other than a suit. He had on a pair of brown suede pants with a matching brown suede hoodie. It wasn't even that cold outside.

"If I leave, how are you going to get Phoebe back?"

I'm about to go to jail!

"If you took my baby, I am going to kill you."

"I like when you show your feisty side. You are so sexy. Phoebe is fine. When we land back in Atlanta on Sunday night, the first stop we will make is to pick her up."

He thinks I'm playing.

I reached into my tote and pulled out my pink nine-millimeter gun.

Roman

Brittany stood in front of me with a gun pointed at my chest, and I could not stop my dick from swelling in my jeans. Obsesia mea (my obsession) was the prettiest woman in the world. There was not another woman in heaven, hell, or Earth that could hold a candle to the woman standing in front of me.

"Baby, if you shoot me, you will never know where Phoebe is. How about I place a call and show you that Phoebe is alive and being spoiled rotten? Then, I need you to run upstairs and pack a bag. We have a flight to catch."

"Roman, I want my baby."

"I promise you she's okay. I have not lied to you yet, and I do not plan to do so. Lower the gun, baby. We really need to get going. I can tell you are stressed out. Let me cater to you this weekend."

Brittany bit her bottom lip. I could tell she was trying to decide if she was going to shoot me or lower the gun to do as I asked.

"You get on my fucking nerves. Call now. I want to see Phoebe with my own eyes," she fussed before lowering the gun. She put the nine-millimeter back inside her tote.

I scrolled down my contact list until I found Kofi's name and hit the video button. Kofi answered a few seconds later, with Phoebe sitting on his lap. He was using one of his hands to rub Phoebe on top of her head. Brittany walked beside me to look at my phone screen. She watched her cat for a couple of minutes before she nodded, giving me the approval to disconnect the phone call.

"Where are we going? And why can't you take me shopping for new clothes when we get there?"

"It is a surprise, but it will be cold, so pack accordingly. On our next trip, I will fly you wherever you want to go and buy you whatever you desire, but there are not any clothing shops where we are going today."

Brittany frowned but refrained from asking any more questions. She turned around and jogged out of the living room and up the stairs. I walked back over to her couch and sat back down. Brittany had a decent three-bedroom brick house. She had enough money in the bank to purchase herself something bigger, but I guess she wanted to start off small. Soon, we will be married, and she will be living with me. She just did not know it.

I expected Brittany to take her time packing her bags, but she returned ten minutes later, ready to go. She had changed clothes and was now wearing a white hoodie and some black leggings. The leggings she had on were not like the leggings she wore in the office during our last session. These were thicker and meant for colder weather. In her hand was a beige-colored suitcase.

I reached out to grab it from her before walking out of the house. Brittany followed me and made sure her house door was locked. By the time she made it to my car, her suitcase was already in the backseat next to the one I had packed last night, and I was holding the passenger side door open for her. Thirty minutes later, we walked through the airport to get to the private section where Constatin's jet was waiting.

Brittany

Exhaustion won, and I fell asleep as soon as the pilot announced it was time for lift-off. It was not until I felt hands on my shoulders, shaking me gently, that I woke up. I lifted my head off Roman's shoulder and looked around with hazy eyes until I remembered where I was.

"We are about to land in a few," Roman told me. It was dark outside the airplane window, and the night sky was lit up with stars. The scene was breathtakingly beautiful.

"Where is the restroom?" I asked.

"Straight to the back. It is the first door on the left."

Roman had my tote in his lap. He must have grabbed it when I fell asleep to keep it from falling. I reached out to pick my tote up before standing and walking to the small restroom. In the restroom, I dug inside my tote and pulled out my small travel bag with my toothbrush and toothpaste in it. After brushing my teeth, I felt more awake, but I had so many questions swirling around in my head. The main one was, why didn't I shoot

Roman? If he had been anybody else, I would have pulled the trigger. Phoebe was the only thing in my life to which I had any kind of emotional attachment.

Is she?

Then, it was the fact that I let this man fly me out on a private jet, and I had no idea where we were. Roman had never lied to me before, but that didn't mean much, especially because we had only known each other for a few weeks. Benjamin crossed my mind, and I knew I should feel something over his death, but people die every day. It was a part of life.

"What are you doing, Brittany?" I questioned myself while looking in the mirror.

Roman had me acting all out of character, but it was like I couldn't stop it. Truth be told, I wasn't sure if I wanted to stop whatever was going on between us. After a couple of deep breaths, I put everything I pulled out back inside my tote and exited the bathroom.

The jet we were on was luxurious, not that I expected anything less from a billionaire. As I walked back down the hallway toward the seats, I took in more of my surroundings. If we had more time, I would have indulged in some of the alcoholic beverages sitting on top of the black and white marble bar.

"Are you okay?" Roman asked me when I sat back down.

"Yes. Where are we?"

"In Northern Canada."

Canda? I am glad I took his warning seriously and packed nothing but winter clothes.

The pilot announced our arrival on the intercom, ending our conversation. We landed a few minutes later. The flight attendant and pilot ended up coming from the front of the plane to where we were to see if we needed any help, but we only had two suitcases, and Roman had both. When we stepped off the plane, we were at another airport, and it was cold as fuck. The temperature had to be in the twenties or lower.

"There is a driver here waiting to take us out to the ocean."

Ocean?

"When you say ocean? Do you mean as in a big body of water? I can't swim."

Roman threw his head back and laughed. I liked how his laugh sounded. It was deep but full of happiness at the same time. Was it possible to own a person's laugh?

"Baby, it would be dangerous for us to swim anyway. We would freeze to death. Do not worry. Neither of us will be jumping in the ocean, nor will I let anything happen to you."

"I don't trust you," I informed him as we walked through the Canadian airport. For it to be nighttime, the airport was swarming with people rushing to make their flights.

"You trust me to a certain extent, or you would not be here with me. I am confident that by the time we get married, you will realize that I only say what I mean, and I do not make empty promises."

Delusional. I have no plans to ever get married.

"Hmmm," I replied.

There was no reason for me to repeat what I had already told him before. If he wanted to believe he could change my mind about marriage, that was on him.

We walked all the way through the airport and outside to a man leaning against a black limousine.

"Mr. Bucur?" he questioned Roman.

"Correct," Roman replied.

The man stood and walked over to us. He took our suitcases from Roman and placed them inside his truck before opening the back door for us. We both slid inside the limousine and got comfortable. Roman joined his left hand with my right one. He used his thumb to rub the backside of my hand. I found the gesture comforting. The windows in the limousine had a dark black tint, making it impossible to see anything outside in the nighttime.

Roman mentioned we were going to be at sea and that there were no shops where we were going. We were either spending the weekend on a secluded island somewhere or on a boat. I got my answer when the limousine stopped. The driver got out and opened the back doors for us. Roman exited the limousine first and held his hand out to help me get out. Imagine my shock when not only was there a yacht waiting for us, but the sky was shining in different colors. I had never seen anything like that in my life. There were blue, green, and even light purple colors swirling around in the sky. It felt like instead of flying to Canada, we had flown to a magical planet in outer space.

Roman

We were in Aurora Village in Yellowknife, Canada. The only requirement I had when I went searching for the perfect weekend getaway for Brittany was that it had to be something rare and unique like she was to me. When I came across the image of northern lights, I knew it was something I wanted us to experience together. The driver took our suitcases out of his trunk and brought them to me.

"I will be back Sunday to drive you two back to the airport. Enjoy your trip," the driver stated.

"Thank you," I replied before digging into my pocket and taking my wallet out. I handed the driver a hundred-dollar bill. He waved goodbye to us and walked back around the limousine to the driver's side.

"Come on, baby."

Brittany had not stopped staring up into the sky yet, but she listened and followed me.

"Good afternoon, Mr. And Mrs. Bucur," the captain of the yacht I rented greeted us as we walked onto the boat.

"Hey," we both replied at the same time. Brittney yawned, still sleepy. She had slept during the flight here, but that was only a couple of hours.

"The yacht has a fully functioning kitchen. I hired two chefs to prepare our meals while we are here. We have our own room with a bathroom attached. Another room has been set up for us to receive couple's massages, yoga, and pedicures tomorrow," I informed Brittany while the captain led us to our stateroom.

"Here you two are." The captain stopped in front of a door before smiling and walking away to give us privacy.

Brittany opened the door, and we walked inside. I took our suitcases and placed them inside the empty closet before walking back over to where Brittany stood. The state room had a spacious layout with a large balcony, a king-sized bed with high-quality linen, a huge walk-in closet, a comfortable seating area, and a mini bar.

"This is nice," Brittany said. She glanced over at me and smiled. The smile was a genuine one, not the one she used when she was masking.

A euphoric feeling spread through my body, and I felt lightheaded. I would give anything to see Brittany smile like that every day for the rest of our lives.

"Why are you staring at me like that?"

"Looking at you makes me happy. Why would I not stare at you every chance I could?"

We gazed into each other's eyes, letting the energy in the air whisper silent feelings that I knew we both felt. It was not until the boat jerked and Brittany stumbled that either of us moved. I reached out and caught her in my arms.

"Why do you always smell so damn good?"

Her voice was low and seductive. I leaned down to place a soft kiss on her forehead before replying.

"My brothers and I have a customized Baccarat sent created a view years ago. Every few months, we pay Francois money to send us bottles of the special Baccarat. We just sent money off for four new bottles last week. Constatin plans to surprise Kofi with his own bottle when they arrive."

"Kofi is the one who has my cat, right? I saw his name on the top of the screen when you FaceTimed him earlier."

"Yes, Kofi is our brother by marriage and our information consultant. Let's go have a quick look outside and then get ready for bed."

Our hands joined together before I led her out of the room and back up to the top of the yacht.

"Omg, are those tents?" Brittany asked.

We were standing near the rails, looking out over the sea. The sky was truly a beautiful sight. Brittany was looking at Aurora village as we sailed through it. There were hundreds of small tents spread out everywhere in the village.

"Yes, people come from all over the world to spend a night under the northern lights. They all sleep in small tents. When we come back, we can stay in the village if you like. I just wanted our first time to be more intimate."

"Roman, all of this is amazing! What made you bring me here?"

"You are rare, Brittany. A diamond in a world full of rhinestones. I wanted our first trip to be someplace rare, like you."

Brittany let my hand go and stepped in front of me. She leaned her head back against my chest, and I wrapped my arms around her body tight.

"I don't date, especially men in the mafia. People assume I just have issues with commitment, but I am a sociopath. I can't give you what you want, Roman."

"You are all I want. Why do you not date men in the mafia?"

"My father used to work for the mafia. What his role was, I am unsure, but I know it involved managing money. He was always gone, and we were never really close, but I do believe he loved me. If I wasn't at school, I was spending time with my mother or my grandmother, who lived with us. Anyway, I was eight years old when I was woken out of my sleep by yelling. I got out of my bed and walked downstairs to see what was going on because my parents had never argued in front of me.

"When I walked into the kitchen, there were three men in suits standing in there with my father. He was begging and pleading with one of the men while the other two men stood back, watching them talk. I called my father's name, and he turned to look at me. He had tears running down his face. It wasn't until I walked further into the kitchen that I spotted my mother and grandmother on the kitchen floor, bleeding. They weren't moving, but there was so much blood leaking from their bodies.

"Before I could ask my father what happened, the man he was arguing with lifted his hand and shot my father in the head. I screamed. The man walked over to me, and I pissed on myself out of fear. He put his gun up and squatted to talk to me. He told me that my father brought this on himself, and if he hadn't been a lying, stealing, piece of shit, he would still be alive. He also told me that a weak person was a dead person, and if I wanted to survive in this cold world, I would learn that disrespect should never be tolerated. The man then used the same hand he killed my family with to wipe my tears, then stood and left. The two men followed them. I stood in the kitchen crying until the sun came back up hours later. Then I walked over to my dead father's body and dug into his pocket to find his cellphone and call the police."

I was quiet while I processed what she said. I knew about her parents and grandmother being killed, but it was classified as a robbery gone bad in her background check.

"If you hate mafia men, why do you counsel them?"

"I don't hate them. I have no feelings toward them at all. If anything, because of my past, I understand how the underground works. My father knew he was putting our family's lives at risk when he stole from the mafia. It was his fault, not theirs. The only thing he did right was put me down as his beneficiary on a million-dollar life insurance policy. When I turned eighteen, I received the money. I used it to put myself through college, buy my car, and put money down on my home."

"I am sorry about your family's death, but I will not stop pursuing you. From the moment I laid eyes on you, I knew you were made for me, Brittany. You are just fighting the inevitable."

Brittany did not respond for several minutes. We stood on the deck in each other's arms, watching the ocean and colorful sky.

"Don't get mad at me if I mess this up. Before I met you, I had no desire to be in a relationship," she whispered.

My eyes closed, and that feeling of euphoria I felt earlier returned. Instead of responding, I spun Brittany around in my arms and kissed her.

Brittany

Our tongues moved in sync against each other. Slowly, they danced together, memorizing each other's tastes and igniting our passion. He grabbed me by my neck and deepened the kiss. Arousal flooded my senses. My pussy walls tightened, and I could feel my pussy secretions wetting my panties. I broke the kiss to moan and catch my breath. Roman pulled me back to him by my neck and kissed me again.

Fuck, if this is how I felt when he kissed me, I can only imagine how I will feel when he puts his dick inside of me.

Roman's hand moved from my neck. He slipped both of his hands under my hoodie and moved them up until he reached my breasts. He grabbed them both roughly before rubbing my nipples. The kiss went on and on until Roman moved his head and took a step back. We both took deep breaths of air.

"It's late. Let's take a shower and get ready for bed," Roman said before reaching down to join our hands together.

Is taking a shower together code for him fucking the shit out of me? It better be.

Roman led me back down into our stale room and to the closet. We both unzipped our suitcases and took out everything we needed for our shower. We laid our night clothes out on the bed, and Roman grabbed my hand again to lead me to the bathroom. He let my hand go and slid the glass shower door open to cut the water on and adjust it to the temperature he wanted. He took my body wash and rag out from my other hand and put it on the bathroom caddy along with his body wash.

"Can I undress you?" he asked when he finished.

"Yes. Can I undress you?

"I belong to you. You can do whatever you want to me."

At that point, my pussy had released so much secretions that I could feel my wetness on my thighs.

Together, we took turns removing each other's clothes. Within a few minutes, we stood before each other naked as the day we were born. My eyes took their time roaming Roman's body from his head down to his toes. The bulge I saw in Roman's pants during our first session was nothing compared to the dick swinging in the air now. His dick was big, thick, and had a slight curve in the middle of it.

When my eyes met his again, they had darkened. He stared at me with an intense look before turning around and stepping into the shower. I followed right behind him.

"Baby, will you bathe me first? When I bathe you, I plan to end up on my knees in front of you with my face buried deep inside your pussy."

I was so turned on that I reached behind him to pick his body wash up and lather some into my rag. Quickly, I scrubbed the whole front of his body clean before turning him around to do the same to his backside.

"Done," I muttered five minutes later.

Roman laughed loudly before taking my rag out of my hand. Briefly, I wondered where his rag was while he rinsed his body wash out of mine and then grabbed my body wash. He squeezed some of my body wash on top of my rag and began to clean my body. Roman took his time bathing me. When he reached my breasts, he used my rag to tease my nipples until they were hard and pointing straight up in the air. He moved the rag away from my nipples and replaced it with his mouth.

"Roman, my nipples still had soap on them," I teased him before ecstasy shot through my body, causing me to moan.

He took turns sucking my nipples and then twisting them until the pleasure became too much to handle, and I pushed his head away. For the first time in my life, I felt like I was about to erupt from a man sucking my breasts. Roman moved the rag back to my body and continued to wash me. When he reached my pussy, I thought he would tease me there like he did with my nipple, but he didn't. Before I knew it, he was turning me around and cleaning my backside.

"Are you a virgin here?" he asked when he wiped between my ass cheeks.

"No, but it has been years since I let anyone stick their dick inside it."

Roman continued washing the rest of my body without saying another word. He didn't speak again until my body had been thoroughly cleaned, and my rag was hanging on the side of the caddy where the hooks were.

"You have to cum in my mouth twice before I will stop eating your pussy."

Roman dropped to his knees in front of me. He picked up my right leg and placed it over his shoulder before burying his whole face in my pussy. He rubbed his face up and down and then left and right, coating his face with my pussy secretions before I felt the first swipe of his tongue.

"Yessssss," I moaned.

Roman's tongue licked both sides of my pussy lips before he moved it up to my clit.

"Ummmmmmm," I whimpered when he sucked my clit into his mouth. He sucked my clit gently with his mouth but flicked his tongue roughly up and down against it. My eyes rolled to the back of my head.

"Grab my hair, baby. Make me stay still until you cum in my mouth."

Roman only had a small piece of hair that was long enough to grab, but I did as he asked. He rewarded me by sliding two of his long ass fingers inside my pussy and moving them in and out of me.

Pleasure began to build from the tips of my toes and moved up through my whole body.

"Your pussy is getting tighter. My good girl is about to explode. Ask me if you can cum, Brittany."

There was something about the way his voice deepened that had me reacting before thinking.

"Roman, can I please cum in your mouth?" I begged.

I thought Roman was eating my pussy good before, but that man turned into the cookie monster. He stopped finger fucking me and moved his hands to my hips to hold me still while licking and sucking my clit until I couldn't think straight.

"Babyyyyyy!" I cried out. My body shook, and my pussy secretions coated Roman's mouth, nose, and eyes.

"Good girl. You did so good," he praised me while I struggled to catch my breath. Roman began to place small kisses all over my pussy, and it was all just too much.

"Roman, I can't handle any more tonight. I am ready to go to bed."

My voice sounded so husky and weak. Roman turned me around, and I frowned.

What the hell is he doing?

Roman slid his warm, thick ass tongue inside my asshole.

"Oh, my god." I huffed. Tears were now falling down my face. I reached out to hold onto the bathroom wall.

He slid his tongue in and out. Pleasure was beginning to build in my body again, but this time, I felt pain mixed in. It created a feeling so intense that darkness began to cloud my vision.

"Are you going to continue being my good girl, or will you be naughty?" Roman asked.

I shook my head up and down and then left to right, delirious from the sensations my body was feeling. One of Roman's hands lightly moved up my thigh and between my legs. He put his thumb on my clit and began to rub. My body went into a trance, and I let the darkness completely take over.

Roman

Brittany came again and passed out. I scooped her into my arms and carried her out of the shower. There were already towels and rags provided to us in the bathroom closet, but I grabbed the one Brittany brought with her and dried her body off with it. When I finished drying her off, I tossed the towel on the floor and carried her out of the bathroom. My dick was hard to the point that every step I took toward the bed hurt, but I wanted to make love to Brittany under the northern lights. I laid Brittany on the bed and then walked around the other side to climb in. My arms pulled her body into mine, and I closed my eyes and fell asleep.

The next morning, I woke up with her still in my arms, asleep. For a while, I just watched her. It was not until my phone rang that I decided it was time for us to get up and get our day started.

"Obsesia mea (my obsession), it's time to wake up," I whispered into her ear. I placed kisses all over her face until I saw her eyes open.

"Move," she fussed, and I laughed.

I placed a kiss on top of her lips before rolling over and climbing out of bed. My phone was still in my pants pocket in the bathroom, and that is where I went. While I was in there, I picked up all our clothes off the floor and carried them all out with me. Brittany was sitting up in the bed with one of the sheets wrapped around her body when I came out.

"If you ever eat another woman out the way you ate me out last night, I will slice your tongue off," she threatened me.

"Good morning to you too, my love," I replied, chuckling.

Brittany did not join me in laughing, but it was because she was serious.

She still cannot see the hold she has over me. Eventually, she will understand that she was the only woman I wanted.

I dug inside my pants pocket and grabbed my phone before placing all the clothes inside a laundry bag in the bathroom closet. Brittany climbed out of bed and went into the bathroom closet to get her suitcase.

Should we take another shower together this morning? No, I will not be able to control myself if I get too close to Brittany's naked body.

The call earlier was from my brother Constatin. I called him and put the phone on speaker. The phone rang a few times before he answered.

"What?" I asked.

"Ari wants to know if Brittany is coming to the baby shower. I asked her during one of our sessions, and she said yes, but my beautiful, easily aggravated wife wanted to make sure."

I wonder if Brittany wants kids?

"Yes, tell I am positive I will be attending," Brittany stated as she walked out of the closet.

"Thank you, girl. I am so ready to get this baby out of me," Ari replied. I should have known she was right there listening to the whole conversation.

"Bye, sister. Me and my wife have plans."

Ari burst out laughing while I hung up the phone.

"You better stop telling everybody I am your wife. People are going to start believing your crazy ass."

"Brittany, we will get married soon."

She froze and then looked up at me. "Baby steps, Roman. We have to take baby steps."

We can take baby steps, teenager steps, or adult steps, but we will be taking them on the way down our wedding aisle. Hell, I would even carry her to the officiant if that is what she preferred.

"How do you feel about us having kids?"

"Roman, you are a psychopath, and I am a sociopath. You know the chances of us having any normal kids are slim, right?"

"Still, the question remains."

"I don't know, but I am currently on birth control. I like having all the attention on me, but maybe one day, that will change. I'm going to take my shower and get ready for the day," she muttered.

That was not a no, which means it is a yes. I just have to do a lot of begging and pleading.

Brittany walked her beautiful ass past me and toward the bathroom. Her ass jiggled with every step she took. I wondered if I could talk her into getting my name tattooed on her ass cheeks. She had to get the yellow eagle tattoo done on her neck anyway. My phone rang again, and I answered it when my mama's (mother) face appeared on the screen.

"Fiul (son), how is the trip?"

"Mama, the trip is beautiful. My woman is mesmerizing."

"You boys make me so proud. Who knew you all would find love right behind each other. Your tata (father) would be so proud."

When my tata was murdered, my mama could not talk about him without breaking down. She was getting stronger every day, but I could still see the hurt in her eyes whenever I went to visit her.

"Yes, Mama, he would be. Constatin just called me to make sure Brittany was attending the baby shower. Are you through planning it?"

Kenya and Ari had helped my mother's healing journey a lot. They always found ways to keep her happy and busy. Even though it was their baby shower, my mother planned most of it. The only input they had was on the colors of the event and what food items they wanted on the menu.

"Yes, everything is done. I love you, fiul (son). Tell my fiiul (daughter) I said, hey."

I will, Mama (mother). I love you, too," I replied before hanging up the phone."

My brothers liked to tease and call me a mama's boy, but the truth was, my father told my mother that I killed those security guards. When she found out, she thought it was because she had done something wrong. I had to explain to her that I killed them because I wanted to, and she had nothing to do with it. Me, her, and my father had agreed not to tell my brothers, or they would have been watching me all day, and that would have really sent me on a killing spree.

I did not get the big deal. If you ask me, my whole family was serial killers, but my father told me the difference was they only killed when it was related to the mafia or family, and I killed because I wanted to watch people die and burn. A killing is a killing, but whatever. I did not care about being labeled a serial killer. Nonetheless, my mother clung more to me after that conversation. She still felt like she had done something wrong and thought if she showered me with extra love, it would fight the need I would get to kill. It did not, but I would never tell her.

I stood and put my phone down on the nightstand. While Brittany took her shower, I took all our clothes out of our suitcases and hung the items up. I put the rest of the items that were left in the suitcase where they needed to go. When I heard the water in the shower shutting off, I had just finished sorting everything out and was ready to take my shower. Brittany walked out of the bathroom dressed in some blue jeans and a soft pink long-sleeved shirt. On her feet were a pair of pink and green tennis shoes. My dick began to grow and thump against my leg.

Calm down, boy. Tonight, you will get what you want.

Brittany's eyes lowered to my dick. Now, I was all the way hard.

Brittany sauntered over to stand in front of me and stood on her tip toes to give me a kiss. Her mouth tasted like mouth wash and sin. I had to have the strength of Doctor Bruce Banner because I broke the kiss after only a few seconds. I went to move around her when she reached out to stop me. Brittany dropped down to her knees in front of me and pulled out a small travel-sized container of mouthwash from her back pocket.

"Baby, what are you doing?"

Brittany opened the mouthwash and poured some in her mouth before placing the travel-sized container on the floor beside her. She swished the mouthwash around her mouth a few times before she reached out with both of her hands to grab my dick.

"Baby...

I was trying to ask her again what was going on, but she put my dick in her mouth, and the icy cool sensation made me forget the words I was about to speak. Brittany sucked on my tip, and I groaned. Her tongue twirled around the head of my dick before she pushed her head forward and swallowed my whole nine inches.

"Damn, you really are my naughty girl, huh? Are you going to suck my dick until I nut? When I nut, you have to swallow all of it like a good girl."

Brittany nodded with her throat full of my dick and began to move her head back and forth. She was sucking my dick so good that I could feel her saliva flowing down the inside of my thighs. I reached out to grab a handful of her hair.

"Naughty girls get punished," I warned her before ramming my dick in and out of her mouth and down her throat.

There was no way in hell she had any gag reflex because each time my dick slid down her throat, I held it there for a few seconds before moving, and she did not make any gagging noises.

"Shit, I am about to nut," I moaned before I felt the nut shoot out the top of my dick and into her mouth. I jerked while filling her mouth with my cum.

When I slid my dick out of her mouth, I had to lean over on the bed to stop myself from falling. Brittany stared me right in the eyes, opened her mouth to show me all the cum I had just deposited inside it and then swallowed every drop.

She already owned my heart and soul; I did not know what more she wanted from me, but when I regained strength in my legs, I walked over to the nightstand and picked my phone up. I logged into my bank account and sent a million-dollar payment to the account I had on file to pay for my psychiatrist visits. On my way into the bathroom to take my shower, I heard Brittany's phone ding, and then she burst out laughing. I could not help but smile as I started the water.

Brittany

Maybe having a boyfriend wasn't as bad as I thought it would be. Today was amazing. After I treated my man to slow head, he took his shower and got dressed. When we exited the state room, we walked back up to the deck. The colors in the sky were gone, and it looked like a normal blue sky.

"Will the colors return tonight?" I asked Roman.

"Yes, it will begin to return after sunset. By ten o'clock tonight, all the colors will be visible like they were last night."

Just thinking about how beautiful it looked blew my mind. Roman really did his big one with this trip. For the rest of my life, I will always think about this weekend. We did not stand in the salon for more than a few minutes before two people came toward us and led us to a room that turned out to be a spa-like cabin.

"Did you know I had a massage scheduled for today?"

"No, surprisingly, I did not."

The couple stopped not too far from us. We greeted them, and they instructed us to take everything off from the waist up. Without hesitating, I began to undress. I did not feel shame or embarrassment. I could get butt-naked in the middle of a party without blinking an eye.

"The chef texted me that he was preparing lunch for us because we missed breakfast. The crew is sailing the boat. The only people here to see what belongs to me are the two people standing in front of me. I would hate for one of them to get a glimpse of your breasts. I will stab them in the eye to make sure they never see a glimpse of anything else again."

The couple's eyes got big before they quickly turned around to give us privacy.

And people thought sociopaths were worse than psychopaths.

Things might have gotten off to a rocky start with the massage therapist, but they eased all the tension and stress right out of my back. It felt so good that I ended up falling asleep in the middle of the massage. My man woke me up when it was over. He helped me off the massage table and put my shirt and bra back on. Then, he led me over to a set of black massage chairs, and I had a seat. Roman squatted in front of me and removed my tennis shoes and socks. While he did that, I watched as the two massage therapists kissed each other and then reached down under their table where the cabinets were. Before they started our messages, they did the same thing and pulled out a bunch of different oils, etc.

How many items do they have down there?

They pulled out two big wooden pedicure spa bowls and brought them over to us. Roman took a seat on the chair beside me and leaned down to remove his shoes and socks. Within minutes, the couple had the bowls full of steaming hot water and whatever clear stuff they poured inside it. The lady squatted, picked up my feet, and put them one by one into the pedicure bowl. A sigh escaped my mouth because it felt amazing. The water was hot but not so high that it took away from the experience. I glanced over at Roman, and the man was doing the same to him.

"Are you getting color put on your toes too?" I asked him.

In today's world, a lot of men wore fingernail polish on their hands and feet. Some people in society didn't like it, but I couldn't care less what people decided to do with their fingers and toes. If it made them happy, that was their business.

"No, I was not planning on it, but I will if you get a property of Roman Bucur tattooed on your ass cheeks."

I looked into Roman's face to see if he was serious, and he was. In college, I had been dared a few times to get a tattoo, and I did it. It didn't even hurt.

"No deal."

"Baby, please. I will get you whatever you want."

You are going to do that anyway.

"How about you get 'Property of Brittany' tattooed on your chest, and I will get 'Property of Roman' tattooed on my arm."

"Are you serious?"

"It's just a tattoo. It's not a big deal."

"We must go get a yellow eagle tattooed on your neck anyway. We can get them done then."

Constatin and Ari both had a yellow eagle tattooed on them. I didn't think much of it until the day Roman came into my office. He had tattoos all over his body, but the first one I noticed was the yellow eagle tattoo on his neck.

"Does it have to do with the underworld?"

The couple was busy giving us a pedicure, but I knew better than to discuss illegal matters in front of people, even if it appeared they weren't listening.

"Correct," he replied before winking at me.

We both decided to get clear paint on our toes. After the pedicure was over, lunch was served to us on the patio. We ate cod au gratin, poutine, and Bannock. The combination was different because, technically, the potato was the main item of two of the dishes, but it was delicious. The fish in the cod au gratin was my favorite because it was cooked to perfection under the crusted cheddar cheese. We still had a couple of hours to waste before it was dark enough outside to see the northern lights, so we decided to go back to our room and watch a movie together. The chef brought our dinner to the room, and we ate a medium wagyu steak, asparagus, and garlic mashed potatoes.

When the movie ended, we took a shower and changed it to our night clothes. We thought it would be a good idea for us to cuddle together in one lawn chair and sleep under the Northern Lights. An image of me sliding from the deck floor into the deep water crossed my mind, but I was not going to let it stop me from having a once-in-a-lifetime experience. We gathered all the covers off the king-sized bed and left the room. When we reached the deck, I paused to look up at the sky. Tonight, the green and blue colors had blended and created a teal color. The sky was teal and light purple. Roman laid all the sheets except the top cover on the lounge chair. He then sat on the chair and lay back.

"Come on, baby." He motioned with his hands for me to climb on top of him.

I climbed on top of him and snuggled into his chest. We both had on long sleeved night clothes, but the wind was blowing ferociously. Roman leaned down to place a soft kiss on my forehead before wrapping his arms around me tight.

"I never thought I would meet someone who I enjoyed more then I enjoyed killing, but being in your presence calms my soul," Roman whispered.

"Roman, I don't know if I have a soul, but what I do know is that you belong to me."

"Correct, and you belong to me."

We let silence take over as we both gazed into the pretty night sky. Roman was the first person I ever had the desire to claim. I warned him that I could be calm, obsessive, and possessive over my property. Let's pray he took my warning seriously before the body count of Atlanta rose significantly. Roman's hand slipped into the bottom of my pajama pants and inside my panties. He pinched my clit before rubbing on it until I moaned. Every time Roman touched my body, it felt like I was about to catch fire. He moved a hand down a little lower and pushed one of his fingers into my pussy. My pussy secretions made a swooshing sound as he finger fucked me. When he stopped, he pulled his hand out of my panties and lifted the finger he'd just had inside my pussy to his mouth. He sucked on his finger until there wasn't any more of my secretions left.

"Take off your pants and panties. I want you to ride my dick under the northern lights."

His voice had gotten lower and sounded raspier. I lifted off his lap and pulled my pants and panties down like he asked. He took them from me and tossed them on the lounger next to us. Roman helped me sit up and move back enough off his lap for him to unzip his pants and reach inside them to pull his dick out. I reached down and grabbed his dick with both of my hands. I hawked a glob of my spit on his dick and used it to jack him up and down.

"Stop teasing me. I want to feel your tight ass pussy lips wrapped around my dick now." His voice was still low, but now he sounded harsher.

It was so sexy that I leaned forward and bit his bottom lip. Roman grabbed a handful of my hair and pulled me up until I was high enough in the air to position his dick at the entrance of my pussy. We made eye contact while I pushed my pussy down, swallowing his dick inside me inch by inch. Once I had him fully inside me, I squeezed my pussy walls tight and moaned from the pleasure that shot through my body.

"You're so beautiful, Brittany. Ride my dick like a good girl."

I moved my hips back and forth, riding his dick slowly. The curve in his dick was hitting my g-spot. My pussy secretions were making a mess of his pants and the cover. My hips did small circles on his dick until I saw him bite his bottom lip to keep from making any noise.

Finish him.

I put both of my feet flat on each side of his body before leaning forward and placing both hands flat on his chest. I used my hands and feet to push my body up and down on his dick.

"Fuck, you're being naughty, Brittany. You know how good

that pussy is between your legs. You're trying to use the sweet ass pussy to control me. The joke is on you, though, because that pussy owns me just like I own that pussy."

Roman reached between my legs and slapped the top of my clit.

"Yessssss," I whimpered. The people on the boat had to hear us fucking. I hoped they were up and watching while masturbating as I rode my man's dick until we both erupted.

Roman reached into his pocket and pulled something out. It wasn't until I heard the flicker and saw the flame that I knew what it was. He brought his lighter close enough to my right nipple that I could feel the heat from the flame.

"Tell me you belong to me."

I shook my head no and bounced my pussy up and down on him faster. Roman moved the flame directly on top of my right nipple, and I screamed. He let the flame burn my nipple for about fifteen seconds before moving it away.

"Good girl. You did so good. Stop being naughty, and I will not have to punish you."

He moved the flame to my left nipple but stopped before burning me with it like he did the right nipple.

"Tell me you belong to me."

"Fuck no."

Roman burned my left nipple with the flame from his lighter, and I erupted into a million pieces. I thought the orgasm he gave me with his mouth was intense, but it had nothing on the feeling of an electric wave flowing through my veins as I soaked his dick with my secretions. Roman growled and tossed the lighter on the floor. He grabbed my body into his arms and stood up rapidly. I wrapped my arms around his neck to stop myself from falling. Roman lowered my body to the ground, turned me around, and pushed the top of my body into the deck chair. My ass was high in the air.

"You are being naughty, baby girl."

Roman smacked me on each ass cheek until they burned from the pain.

"Hmm, you still won't tell me what I want to hear. Naughty, naughty girl."

Roman shoved his big ass dick into my pussy and fucked me like a forty-dollar whore off Las Vegas Boulevard. My ass clapped every time he shoved his dick in and out of me. Pain and pleasure were both hitting me back-to-back.

"Please, Roman, please," I begged him.

"Are you ready to be my good girl? Use your words to tell me what I want to hear, and I will let you cum on your dick again."

"Fuck. Okay, Roman. I belong to you, fuck!" I screamed.

I heard the flickering sound again. Roman slowed down fucking me. He now moved in and out of me at a snail's pace, making sure his dick hit my G-spot every time. My legs started to shake, and I gazed into the sky at the teal and blue swirling together.

"Now, Brittany, cum on your dick, NOW!" Roman ordered and put the flame from his lighter on top of my clit. A tsunami took over my body, and I came over and over until my whole body fell flat on the chair.

"I belong to you, too, baby girl," Roman whispered into my ear and filled my pussy with his nut.

Roman

The next morning, I woke up and carried obsesia mea (my obsession) back to the state room and to the bathroom. I ran us a bubble bath. While the water filled, I placed kisses all over her face to wake her up.

"What time is it?" she asked when she opened her eyes.

"Almost eleven in the morning. We are about to take a bath together, eat lunch, and then depart.

She nodded in agreement, clearly still tired from the lovemaking session we had last night. I stood and put her in the bubble bath first. She scooted up and waited for me to climb inside before leaning back against my chest.

"Did you enjoy yourself?" I asked as I lathered a rag full of her body wash.

"Yes. Did you?"

"It was the best trip I have ever taken, and I have traveled a lot."

I gently used the rag to wash her body, making sure not to touch her nipples or her clit. When I finished, she took the rag from me and turned around to clean my body.

"Stand up, baby," I told her when she finished. She did as I asked and stood.

I let the water out of the tub before grabbing Brittany by the neck and pulling her to me for a kiss. I kissed her passionately and let the love I felt inside for her show without telling her the words because I knew she was not ready to hear how deeply in love I had fallen with her.

A couple of minutes passed before I broke the kiss. We both got out of the tub and dried off. Over the next hour, we got dressed, cleaned up the room, and packed all our belongings. The chef texted me right at one p.m. and told me lunch was ready. Together, we walked hand in hand to the salon and sat at the table to enjoy our last meal on our small getaway. The chef had done as I asked and went with a simple meal. We had chicken Caesar salad and Tortellini soup. By the time we finished, we had made it back to the port. I told Brittany to stay seated while I walked to the room to grab our suitcases. When I came back out, the captain and crew had lined up together to wave goodbye to us. We thanked them for their hospitality and walked off the yacht. The same driver who took us there was leaning against his limousine, waiting for us.

"Good afternoon, Mr. and Mrs. Bucur. How was the trip?" he asked.

"It was amazing," I replied.

The driver nodded and reached out to take the suitcases from us. He put the suitcases in the trunk and walked around to open the right back seat door for us. I reached down to grab Brittany's hand, led her to the right side of the limousine, and watched as she climbed inside. I climbed in behind her, and the driver shut the door.

"As soon as we land in Atlanta, we will go straight to Kofi's house to get Phoebe before I drop you off at home. I will not make it to our session in the morning. We have a commercial about to air, announcing a new collaboration, and I need to go in to work early to make sure everything is prepared."

"Okay."

She gave me one of her rare genuine smiles and leaned her

head on my shoulder. The ride to the airport was silent but comfortable. Brittany went straight to sleep after we boarded the jet and sat down. In a few months, I would find some new rare place for us to visit and surprise her with another trip.

The trip home took about an hour and forty-five minutes. I waited until our pilot landed before waking Brittany up. It was already six in the afternoon, and I wanted my baby to get a full night of rest when she got home.

"Wake up, baby. We must go."

Brittany opened her eyes and yawned. She stretched her arms out wide and stood. I grabbed our suitcases, and we exited the plane. My Bugatti was in the airport parking lot. We just had to make it through the airport, and it took longer than I wanted because of how packed it was.

My car was a welcome sight. I opened the passenger side door for Brittany and waited until she was in and buckled up before closing the door and putting our suitcases in the backseat. Like I promised, I drove straight to Kofi's house to pick up Phoebe. Phoebe jumped out of Kofi's arms and ran to Brittany when Brittany called her name. Brittany picked her up and thanked Kofi for watching her. We left shortly after, and I drove Brittany home. I took her suitcases into the house and up the stairs to her bedroom.

"How many times have you been inside my house?" she asked when I came back down the stairs.

"A few times, baby," I replied before giving her a kiss on the forehead. "Call or text me before you go to bed tonight."

"Hmmmmm," she replied, but I knew she would listen. I gave her one more kiss on the forehead and walked out of her house.

How am I going to convince her to move in with me?

I pondered the question as I pulled out of her driveway and headed toward my home.

Brittany

Roman: I miss you

Brittany: Roman, you took me out to eat last night and ate my pussy in the bathroom.

Roman: It is not my fault you taste sweeter than anything they were serving on the menu.

Brittany: Bye. I have one more client coming in for the day. Plus, we already have plans to take your mother grocery shopping on Saturday.

Roman: If you would move in with me, we would not have to spend another night apart from each other.

I shook my head before exiting from the message Roman had sent me. We had only been going together for three weeks, and he had been pleading with me to move in with him. It was too soon. I told him we needed to take baby steps. Roman hated to hear the word 'no' coming from my lips. When we came back from Canada, we decided that it would be best for me to stop seeing him as a client. It would have been different if we were just fucking around on the low, but we were in a relationship.

Constatin was the first person he told, and his brother was so happy to learn we were together that he no longer gave a fuck about his sessions. I would be lying if I said Roman didn't still need psychiatric help, but one of the first things I learned in college was that you could only help the patients who wanted to be helped. At least he hadn't murdered anybody else since he killed Benjamin and set his house on fire. Someone knocked on my office door, interrupting my thoughts.

"Come in," I yelled before setting my notebook and pen on my desk.

Greg walked into my office, and I cringed inside. He had been trying his best to come on to me, but I had been ignoring all his advances. Roman killed all the desires I had to sleep with multiple people. Greg closed my office door and took a seat in the chair in front of my desk.

"How can I help you?" I asked.

"Ms. Gabriele, you have been working for me for three years, and I thought you took your job seriously. Unfortunately, I don't know if I can keep you working here in my clinic much longer."

What the fuck?

"Greg, what in the hell are you talking about?"

Greg smirked, and I felt my temper rising. I had too many other tasks to complete to play silly mind games with a man who couldn't outsmart me on his best day.

"Sleeping with a client, Brittany. Is he the reason you ended our situation? How much is he paying you to spread your whoreish legs wide open for him?" he spat.

"Greg, I don't know how many times I have to tell you that resorting to such vulgar language for a man credited as one of the best psychiatrists in Atlanta is truly disappointing. I am not sleeping with any clients. Whoever you got your information from misinformed you."

He jumped out of his seat and stormed around my desk to point his finger in my face.

"You lying bitch. I pulled up to your house last night to surprise you and saw you kissing that Bucur boy on your porch. His hands were all over you."

"Greg, first, back the fuck up. You are being hostile, and I will kill you and do the time for it. Second, that 'Bucur boy,' as you so rudely put it, is no longer my client. He hasn't been my client in weeks because we decided to pursue a relationship. Last, how the hell are you going to accuse me of using my pussy to fuck a client when you, the boss, used to fuck my pussy anytime I let you. What do you think will happen if I report it to the board?"

Greg's face turned bright red with anger.

How in the world did the man become a psychiatrist when he throws temper tantrums like a five-year-old?

"I wish I never put my dick inside you."

The dick wasn't even good enough for you to be throwing it in my face.

"No, you wish you could put your dick inside me again. Seriously, this is childish behavior, Greg. You had no business coming by my house unannounced late at night. You hurt your feelings. I suggest you get the hell out of my office and figure out how to process them."

"You are fired. I want you out of here NOW!" he yelled.

I enjoyed the clients I worked with, but it was definitely time for me to find a new place to work. Hell, my bank account had a million and a half dollars in it. I could open my own damn psychiatric clinic.

"Thank you for the job opportunity," I replied.

I stood to start packing my stuff while Greg looked at me in shock. He expected me to beg him to keep my job when if he had been paying attention with his eyes instead of that weak ass dick in his pants, he would have known Brittany didn't do any begging.

"If you give me thirty minutes, I will have all my stuff packed and a letter of resignation sent to your email."

"Brittany, you don't have to do this. I apologize. You were right. I let my emotions get the best of me. We can go back to how things used to be between us. Don't pretend like we didn't have a good time together."

Is it crack? What the hell was wrong with this man?

I opened my mouth to cuss him out, but he grabbed my face and pressed his lips to mine.

"What the hell is going on here?" I heard a male voice that caused my body to freeze.

Roman

I was already on the way to Brittany's job with a vase of blue roses when I messaged her and told her I missed her. Every week, I made sure she got a new vase of roses delivered to her job. I was surprised when she did not ask me about them in our messages, but I knew she only had a couple hours left to work today before she could leave and go home.

The last few weeks had flown by, and I had enjoyed every day of them. If Brittany and I were not spending time together, we would talk on the phone until she fell asleep. Brittany told me I had become codependent on her, and I did not argue because she was right. But what she did not realize was that she was just as codependent on me as I was on her. The other night, I had to go to a meeting at Constatin's house about one of the underbosses getting busted by the Feds and snitching. The underboss was in protective custody, but he should have known better than to trust the police.

Constatin said Vincent planned to handle it personally, but if he needed us to help with the situation, he would let us know. Once I made it home and showered, I passed out as soon as my head hit the pillow. I wasn't asleep for more than thirty minutes when I was woken by someone banging on my door. Brittany's crazy ass was outside my house with her pink gun in her hand, talking about she called me ten times, and I would not answer the phone because I was cheating on her.

Instead of arguing, I told her to bring her ass on in the house and get in the bed with me. She walked through every room in the house, checking closets and under beds, before she finally realized I was telling her the truth. She did not even apologize; she just stripped naked and climbed into my bed like she did the first time she slept over after one of our date nights.

I pulled into her job parking lot and turned my car off. She was going to pretend that I was getting on her nerves by being there but would fuss when it was time for me to leave. It was crazy how we had only been dating for a few weeks, but I felt like I had known her all my life. I reached over to pick up the vase of roses and got out of my car. When I entered the psychiatric clinic, the secretary's eyes got big.

"Good afternoon. Do not worry about calling Brittany to let her know I'm here," I told her.

"Wait, sir," she called after me, but the sound of yelling had me walking faster toward my baby's office.

I opened the door and could not believe what I saw. Brittany and her boss were kissing. Brittany, the woman I planned to marry and spend the rest of my life with, had her lips on a man who was not me. I could not believe it.

"What the hell is going on here?" I yelled.

Brittany froze, but her boss turned his head at me and smiled. I dropped the vase of roses on the floor and pulled my gun from my waist.

Somebody was about to die.

I lifted my gun and pointed it at her boss. He dropped the smile off his face and threw his hands in the air. I heard the secretary's heels clacking as she approached us before she screamed and ran away. My trigger finger went over the trigger, ready to end this motherfucker's life for touching what did not belong to him when Brittany jumped in front of her boss.

"Move, Brittany."

"No, Roman, you can't kill him here. Put the gun up and leave."

My heart felt like someone had taken a knife and cut it out of my chest.

"You protecting him?"

Brittany shook her head from left to right, but she did not move.

"Why were you kissing him, Brittany?"

I felt like less of a man even having to ask her that question. She belonged to me. Her lips had no business on him.

"Roman, I didn't kiss him, but you have to leave now."

Now, she's lying to my face like I do not know what the fuck I just saw.

"Do not insult my intelligence. I know what I saw. You have two choices, Brittany. Move out the way and let me kill your other boyfriend, or watch me walk out of your life for good."

"Roman, leave. You are not thinking rationally right now."

Fuck both of them. If she wanted to protect him after he disrespected me, she could die with him.

Pull it, pull it. Kill them both.

My mind was telling me to pull the trigger, but after a few more seconds passed, I knew my heart would not let me do it.

"You're dead to me, Brittany."

I lowered my gun and turned around to walk right back out of the office.

Brittany

"The person you are calling is unavailable to take your call right now."

I hung up the phone and hit the contact to dial Roman's number again.

"The person you are calling is unavailable to take your call right now."

It took everything in me not to chuck my phone into the wall. Instead, I placed it on the nightstand and stared at the ceiling. I had called Roman's phone over twenty times tonight. At first, the call would ring a few times and then go to voicemail. Now, I just kept getting the same automated phone message.

Girl, you are blocked. Stop calling that man, and move on with your life.

No! I argued with the voice inside my head. There would be no moving on for either of us. Roman belonged to me, and I belonged to him. He was my property; he just needed time to calm down after the mess Greg pulled earlier. I closed my eyes and thought back to the moment when Roman walked out of my office. Well, my former office.

Listen to me because I am only going to say this once. When the police get here, you are goin' to tell them that there is some kind of confusion happening. Your childhood friend from Italy, Rome, Spain, Greece, I honestly don't give a fuck what country you choose, but you better pick one of them motherfuckers. Tell the police whatever name you come up with in that empty ass head of yours. No, as a matter of fact, tell them your childhood friend named John Smith popped up to visit you on his way back out of the country to complete his tour in Germany. You two were joking around, and the secretary thought the joke was serious. She overreacted and dropped my damn vase of roses that she was supposed to deliver to me. Make it sound convincing, Greg, or I will email every member of the board a video of you ramming your weak ass dick inside of me. I will cry wolf and tell them you blackmailed me into having sex with you for years. Do you know how many messages I have of you begging me to let you fuck me? If you don't send the police on their way when they get here without mentioning Roman fucking Bucur's name, I will destroy you and everything you worked hard for.

Greg looked at me in shock. That shock quickly turned into disgust when he saw how serious I was.

"You are one evil ass bitch," he muttered.

"I damn sure am. When the police leave, you better pray to whatever God you believe in that our paths never cross again."

Greg didn't have time to respond because we heard the police sirens. Not even a minute later, two officers walked into the building. Greg jumped into action. He rushed out to shake both of their hands and introduce himself. They told him they got a call from a woman crying hysterically about a man waving a gun. Greg laughed like it was the funniest joke he ever heard in his life. He then went on to explain how the secretary misinterpreted what she saw. The officers asked him a few more questions before they shook hands one more time and left.

The secretary watched the whole scene happen in fear. She kept her mouth shut, though, because if she hadn't, she wouldn't be on God's wake-up call list in the morning. As soon as the officers left, I packed all my stuff up and walked out of the office.

Thoughts of what happened earlier faded away, and I focused

back on the ceiling. Silence surrounded me, and I didn't like how it sounded. I picked up my phone again and tried to call Roman's phone again, but all I got was that damn automated voice message. There were so many other things I should have been focused on, like if I wanted to look for a new job or open my own clinic, but my thoughts kept drifting back to Roman.

I don't know how many more times I tried to call Roman's phone before I convinced myself to get out of my bed and take a couple sips of NyQuil to help me sleep. Within a few minutes of getting back in bed, I felt the medicine kick in, and I got drowsy. The last thing I remember thinking was that Roman should have cooled off by the time I woke up.

"Get up," a voice whispered in my ear.

A hand went around my neck and squeezed tight. I opened my eyes, and there was a man standing over me in a scream mask. I couldn't scream if I wanted to because the man was squeezing the hell out of my neck. After a few more seconds, he let my neck go. I inhaled deeply and then paused.

There are only four men I know who wore that kind of cologne. My man was home.

A smile appeared on my face before the man lifted a needle and plunged it into my neck. Everything went black.

Roman

It was three in the morning, and all Brittany's neighbors were in their beds, sleeping peacefully. Brittany was slung over my shoulder as I carried her down her stairs and out of her house. The medicine I injected into her neck was benzodiazepine. It would not keep her unconscious for long, but I could not risk her saying something stupid before I kidnapped her, or one of us would have ended up dead. My trunk was already open slightly. I lifted it more and tossed Brittany inside. Her head bumped against the bottom of my trunk, and her eyes flew open.

"Roman!"

She started fussing, but I slammed the trunk down, silencing whatever she was about to say. I got back inside my car and hit the button to start it. The woods where my father used to take us to hunt deer and hogs was where I headed. It was the same woods where I killed and burned my first two security guards. The sound of Brittany kicking and punching the inside of my trunk could be heard all the way in the front seat. I turned the radio up and pulled out of Brittany's driveway.

On the drive to the woods, I kept seeing flashes of Brittany and her boss kissing in my mind. I could not get the image out of my head. Even when I tried to sleep, the image popped into my head as soon as I closed my eyes. I ended up getting back out of bed and deciding tonight would be the perfect night for a late-night hunt.

When I made it to the woods, I pulled into them and drove far enough that any car driving by on the highway would not see my car but not far enough that I was a mile deep in the woods. I turned my car off and got out. On my key fob, I hit the unlock button and waited. As I expected, Brittany jumped out of the trunk like a wild animal. She ran toward me, ready to fight, until I pulled my gun from my waist and pointed it at her. Brittany was not afraid of dying, but she knew she had been a naughty girl, and I would punish her for her actions.

"Let's play a little game. You have three minutes to run away from me as far as you can. If I catch you, I will fuck you and leave you in the middle of the woods. If you make it back to the car without me catching you, I will take you home and grant you one final wish."

Brittany stared at me while she thought about what I had just said. Regardless of if she wanted to play or not, she was running her ass into those woods.

"For clarification, the wish can be anything, right?"

"If you make it back to the car without being caught."

"Okay, but we need to talk after this."

After this, there will be nothing left for us to say to each other.

"Your three minutes start now. Run, naughty girl, run."

Brittany took off running. She only had on her pajamas. Her feet were bare and would probably end up getting cut and bruised. She deserved it. Three minutes passed by slowly, and as much as I wanted to take off behind her sooner, I was a man of my word.

"Brittany, where are you?" I yelled into the woods and took off.

Brittany was smart enough to know not to go too far in the woods, or she would have ended up lost, trying to find her way back to the car. No, she was close by, probably watching me.

"Brittany!" I yelled again before standing still to listen.

One of the first lessons of hunting my father taught us was that nature would always point you to the prey. It could be something as simple as a flock of birds flying over a particular area or the sound of a branch breaking when the prey is unaware that they are being hunted. Leaves rustled to the left of me, and I smiled. Calmly, I walked toward the sound until I heard another sound to my right.

I got you, naughty girl.

I faked like I was about to run to the right, just to turn around and run left. Brittany screamed and tried to run deeper into the woods, away from me. It was useless. I had been hunting all my life; there was no escaping me.

"Got you." I laughed when I grabbed the back of Brittany's shirt.

I threw her into the nearest tree and watched as she hit the tree and arched her back in pain.

I leaned down to grab her by her neck and stand her up straight.

"Mask?" she muttered.

"You lost the right to look at me. Dead people cannot see," I replied.

Brittany opened her mouth to talk, but I squeezed her neck tighter. It was not until she brought her hands up to try to pry mine from around her neck that I let her go. She slumped back down to the dirt and took big gasps of air.

"You are such a naughty girl. On your knees where you belong. Too bad I wouldn't let you put your lips on my dick again if they were the last pair of lips on Earth."

"Stop, Roman. You do not mean any of this. You want to punish me for some shit I did not do, then shut the fuck up and punish me, but don't lie to me."

"The audacity of you to think the words coming out of my mouth are anything but the truth."

I reached down, grabbed her by the hair, and pulled her back up before ripping her shirt and bra off. Brittany's nipples were hard, and it made me angry. I leaned down and bit her right nipple until my teeth pierced the skin. Small drops of her blood went into my mouth before I let her go. Brittany had tears forming in her eyes, but she did not scream out in pain.

"Did kissing him make your pussy wet?"

"He kissed me. I did not kiss him."

Instead of replying, I pushed her pajama pants down and ripped her panties off. I put her panties in my mouth, sucked all her pussy juices clean, and then took them out of my mouth and shoved them into hers.

"If that was the case, you should have let me kill him."

I could tell she wanted to respond, but she did not spit her panties out of her mouth.

"It is a little too late to try to be a good girl now. You have been naughty, and naughty girls must be punished."

I unzipped my pants and pulled my dick out of my briefs before reaching out to pick up her left leg. My body went between her legs before I positioned my dick in front of her pussy hole and pushed inside. I hated how much pleasure rushed through my body.

"You have the best pussy I have ever fucked in my life, and trust me, I have fucked a lot of whores just like you."

Brittany's pussy juices flowed out of her and onto both of our legs. I pulled back until only the tip of my dick was left inside her pussy and rammed my dick back inside her. Over and over, I repeated the same action until she was moaning loudly around the pair of panties she had in her mouth.

"Spit the panties out and talk to me like a good girl."

Brittany did as I asked and spit her panties on the dirt. Temptation got the best of me, and I spit in her mouth before joining our lips together. This kiss was not a passionate kiss, but one meant to punish naughty little girls. The kiss did not last long because I moved my head back. My thrusts increased inside her, and I felt my balls tighten. I reached into my pocket and pulled my lighter out. Brittany heard me flick the lighter on because she looked down at the flame. I leaned forward and kissed her on her forehead before moving my lips to her ear.

"I love you, Brittany, and you played with my heart," I whispered into her ear before putting the flame from my lighter over her heart and holding it there to let it burn her skin.

I kept the lighter on her chest until the smell of burned flesh drifted to my nose. My head fell back, and I groaned before pulling out of her and nutting all over her stomach. I let Brittany go and watched her slide back down to the dirt before I turned around and walked back to the car. It took Brittany twenty minutes to find her way to the car. She walked over to the passenger side door, opened it, and got inside. No words were spoken between us. I pulled out of the woods and drove her back home. Instead of pulling into the driveway, I pulled in front and waited for her to get out.

"You really done with me, Roman?"

I did not reply.

She sat there for a few minutes before she opened the door and got out. She walked to her front door with her head held high as if she were not almost naked and badly bruised.

Eleven

Seven days. It had been seven days since the last time I saw Roman Bucur. I felt like someone gave me the best toy in the world and then took it away from me. As a psychiatrist, I knew it was important for me to accept my feelings, determine which feeling was making me feel which way, and then process them in a healthy manner, such as journaling. The issue was, I didn't know how to pinpoint feelings I'd never had before. All I knew was I missed Roman, and I wanted him back in my life.

Other than some light grocery shopping, I hadn't left my home. I hadn't had a big appetite, and the few food items I did buy were still in my refrigerator. My days had been spent reading one of my favorite books, cuddling with Phoebe, or watching one of my favorite TV shows. My hand went to my chest to the burn mark, and I rubbed it. I know it sounded crazy, but the burn mark on my chest was the last thing Roman gave me, and rubbing it gave me a weird sense of comfort.

Kenya and Ari's baby shower was two weeks away, and I had been counting down the days until it arrived. At least I knew when I attended the event, I would get a glimpse of Roman. His mother and I talked on the phone every day. I was honest with her and told her everything that had happened. She told me Roman was letting his pride blind him to the truth and that he would eventually see the light. She told me to let him go and stop trying to reach out to him. That was four days ago, and I hadn't picked up the phone and dialed his number again.

I would often think back to everything that happened the day Greg kissed me, and I didn't regret anything I did. If I were given a chance to change my actions that day, I would decline. My doorbell rang, and I frowned before climbing out of my bed, going down the stairs, and walking to my front door.

"Who is it?" I called out. There wasn't a response.

I peeked through the peephole to see if anyone was there and spotted a bouquet of blue roses on my porch. I opened my door and peered outside. Whoever had delivered them was already gone. There was a letter sticking out the middle of the roses. I squatted, picked the roses up, and brought them into the house. My steps quickened as I walked down my hallway and into my kitchen.

As soon as I placed the bouquet in the center of my kitchen table, I picked up the envelope and lifted it to my nose. The smell of Baccarat floated through my nostrils, and I flashed a real smile. Slowly, I opened the envelope and pulled the letter out. I unfolded the envelope and frowned when I saw a check for twenty million dollars with my name on it. Roman's name was signed on the bottom of the check.

Why did he send me a check for twenty million dollars?

I turned the letter to the side and let the check slide on top of the table so I could read what the letter said.

"Even though things did not work out between us, I will always want the best for you."

Roman signed it with his first and last name. A part of me wanted to tear the check up into several small pieces.

Girl, you sound dumb as fuck. If you don't take yo' dumb ass upstairs to get the keys so we can drive to the bank and deposit this damn check.

Angrily, I snatched the check up and put it inside my tote

before going up the stairs to shower and put on some clothes to head out to the bank.

Roman

"Let me get this straight. You had me deliver a bouquet of roses with a letter and a twenty million dollar check to a woman you claim you don't want anything else to do with?" Kofi asked me.

He and I were in my office at work. He had not returned from his lunch break too long ago when I asked him to make a small detour for me.

"What are you trying to say?"

Kofi laughed before shaking his head.

"Bro, I am going to hold your hand when I say this. You are in love with Brittany. You are in love with Brittany. You are in love with Brittany."

I am confused. He is not even holding my hand. And why did he have to repeat the same thing three times?

"Kofi, I never said I was not in love with Brittany. I said I did not want to be with her."

"Boy, y'all three, I tell ya. Roman, you just gave that woman twenty million dollars. What about that makes you think you are done with her?"

"She cheated on me."

He inhaled and exhaled deeply as if I were getting on his nerves.

"Did you know Brittany and your mother talk every day?"

No. How did he know that, and why did Mama not mention it to me?

"What do they have to talk about?"

"Yo' dumb ass. Turns out Greg had kissed Brittany without her consent. She didn't want that man to kiss her, nor did she encourage it. From what Mama told me, the man was obsessed with her and wouldn't leave her alone after she broke it off with him."

"She should have let me shoot the slimy bastard."

"Roman, you were in the middle of a damn psychiatric clinic, waving a gun and threatening to kill the owner. The secretary had called the police on you. She didn't protect him, idiot. She protected you. You forgot that not everyone knows how many police officers y'all have in y'all pocket, and who's to say if the cop who showed up was dirty or not."

Fuck the police. I would have murdered every one of them if they touched me.

"So, just take her back and forget about her lips being on another man?"

"If the situation were reversed, you would have been raising hell. Mama said you are letting your pride blind you. Forgive that woman, make up, and get married."

"Hmmmm," I replied. Kofi shook his head again before standing and walking out of my office.

The last seven days had been difficult, to say the least. I missed Brittany, but I was also mad at her. The words Kofi had just spoken swirled into my mind. Was I letting my pride turn me into a blind fool? Can Brittany and I move past this? So many questions popped into my head that I ended up laying my head on my desk to ease some of the tension I felt building. Something had to give, and fast before I lost my cool and went on a killing spree.

Brittany

Finally, the day I had been waiting for had arrived. The baby shower was being held at the Nobu Hotel downtown. Kenya was having a girl, and Ari was having a boy, so the theme was Sugar and Spice. The itinerary for the baby shower described a ballroom event with expensive gift-giving. I decided to wear a pink and blue grenadine backless V-neck spaghetti strapped evening gown with silver Giuseppe Zanotti high heels. My hair was flat ironed with a middle part, and I did a natural beat on my face. I got Kenya a pink Moncler diaper bag, and I got Ari a blue one. My eyes scanned my body one more time in the mirror before I turned around to gather the gifts.

A few minutes later, I walked out of my front door. The Nobu Hotel was only a fifteen-minute drive from my house. When I pulled up to the hotel, the first thing I spotted was security everywhere. I parked my car, grabbed the gifts, and got out.

"Invitation." two security guards stopped me at the door.

My invitation was inside my tote. I went to dig in the bag when a male voice behind me spoke up.

"She is with me, guys."

I turned around and smiled when I spotted Kofi behind me. The man had at least twenty gifts in his hands.

"Hey, Kofi, thank you," I replied.

"No problem, follow me. You are sitting at the family table." Kofi walked around and passed security.

We entered the hotel and walked to the ballroom. The gift tables were on the right when we walked inside. Kofi and I walked over there first to set our bags down. Once the gift bags were out of my hands, I glanced around the baby shower. There had to be at least two hundred people in attendance. Mama, well, Roman's mama, had decided to use gold and black colors to decorate, and everything turned out amazing. She had black and gold building blocks that spelled out B-A-B-Y. There were various signs hanging from the ceiling that said, "Oh, baby," in black and gold. All the tables had black tablecloths on them with gold menus, plates, and silverware. It was the perfect balance between elegance and baby shower fun.

"Over here," Kofi stated before walking to a table at the front of the ballroom.

Mama, Kenya, Ari, Constatin, Alexandur, and Roman were seated at the table. There was only one person sitting at the table with whom I wasn't familiar, but I figured she was extended family or a close family friend. I walked around the table to give Mama a hug before walking around to do the same to Kenya and Ari. Kenya and Ari's chairs were situated where they were both at the head of the table with their husbands on the other side of each of them.

"Hey, ladies, you two look amazing," I told them.

Ari was going on eight months, and her stomach appeared as if it could burst open at any given moment. Kenya was only a month behind her, but her stomach was significantly smaller. She looked like she was carrying a big watermelon under her shirt.

I wonder if it is like that because Ari is carrying a boy, and Kenya is carrying a girl.

"Girl, I am so over being pregnant. People pretend that being pregnant is such a beautiful experience. It's a lot of things, but beautiful, especially when you are eight months pregnant, is a bunch of bullshit."

Ari sounded happy and miserable at the same time as she spoke. I was already a selfish person. I couldn't understand why women would want to put themselves through intense pain just to bring another human being into this world. Then, they are responsible for taking care of and raising the human beings they brought into this world for the rest of their lives. How bizarre.

"You don't have long left before you go into labor. One day soon, you will be holding your beautiful baby boy in your arms," I replied.

Ari smiled at me before bursting out crying.

What did I do?

"Baby, calm down. Look at all the nice gifts our baby received. You have to stop crying if you want to see what all our baby got," Constatin stated while rubbing her back.

She looked over at the gift tables that had gifts on top of them, under them, and on the side of them and stopped crying.

"Look at all those presents. I can't wait to see all the stuff he got," she replied happily.

That was my cue to go sit down because the way she went from crying hysterically to smiling happily was giving, "And the Academy Award for best actress goes to..."

There were only two empty seats left at the table, and one of them happened to be right next to Roman. Neither of us had made eye contact yet. I froze, unsure of what to do.

"Fiiul (daughter), your seat is right there next to my son and his date," Roman's mama said.

Date? Roman brought a date?

"Yes, ma'am," I replied. My voice sounded taut and frigid.

Kenya coughed and whispered the word "messy" in the middle of the cough. She and Ari burst out laughing.

I did as Mama said and took a seat next to Roman. My hands shook slightly, and I put them in my lap. I tried to take a few deep breaths in and out to control my temper, but I was pissed. On the itinerary we received with our invites, dinner would be served first, then we would play baby shower games, next the ladies would open some of their gifts, and the night would end with the band playing music for people to dance in the open space in the middle of the ballroom. It would be a miracle if I made it through dinner without injuring someone.

"Roman, are you okay? You haven't said more than a few words all night," his date whispered to him.

Roman did not reply, but I could feel his eyes on me. He knew bringing a date would piss me the fuck off. I reached into my tote and pulled my gun out before setting it on the table. One of the brothers' security guards stepped forward, but Alexandur waved them away.

"Roman, let's play a little game. I have a question, and if you answer the question correctly, I won't shoot you after I finish killing your date."

"Oh shit," I heard Kofi mutter. A few people at the table laughed, but I kept my gaze focused on Roman. He didn't reply.

"Question time. My gun is loaded with ten rounds. How many bullets are going to hit major organs in your date's body when I shoot every one of them into her flesh?" I asked him.

More laughter could be heard at the table, but Roman remained silent.

"You have three minutes to get her the fuck out of here before we all find out the answer to the question," I warned him.

"Roman, are you going to let her talk about me like that? Make her leave!" his date fussed at him.

"I think it might be best if you leave. Brittany is an excellent shot, and she really will fire all ten rounds into your body," Roman turned to his date and said.

"Hell naw. Y'all asses stay wilding." Kofi laughed.

"No, I am not leaving. You brought me here with you, and I am staying. She is the one who needs to leave, Roman," the woman whined.

"She is going to kill you, and I will do nothing to stop her. No one at this table will. Listen to me and leave while you still can."

His date gasped, and I picked my gun back up. I took the safety off and cocked it.

"One minute left. Move out the way, Roman."

Roman shrugged before scooting his chair back.

"Girl, you about to die, and Roman's psychotic ass is going to let you. He only invited you here to make the woman with the gun in her hand mad. Run, girl, run. These people are clinically insane in the brain." Kofi tried to talk some sense into the woman. She crossed her arms like she didn't care about living.

I lifted the gun and focused my aim on the center of her forehead. My trigger finger moved over the trigger, and I began to count down the last ten seconds in my head. Roman waited until there were only a couple of seconds left before he stood and put his body in front of the woman.

Well played, Roman. Well played.

Roman was showing me how he felt when I protected another person who disrespected him.

"What's a mafia baby shower without a little blood getting spilled?" Ari said before she and Kenya laughed again. Everybody except the woman hiding behind Roman was missing some screws in their heads.

"Now, I am jealous. You guys should have sat me at the table where all the fun was," a male voice said, interrupting the moment.

I looked up to see who it was and paused. Not much had changed about the man who killed my family in front of me. He was older now with grey hair, but his face was still the same.

"Vincent, you made it. Have a seat with us," Constatin told the man.

He smiled at Constatin before walking around the table to have a seat in the last empty chair. The man lifted his head and looked at me. We stared at each other.

"Do I know you from somewhere? You look familiar," he said.

"We have met before, but it was a long time ago," I replied.

Roman was staring at me with curiosity in his eyes, but I pretended not to see him. If the man they called Vincent hadn't walked over to the table, I would have shot Roman and his little date.

"When did we meet?" Vincent asked.

"You murdered my family in front of me when I was a little girl. My father worked for you. He stole something from you, and you killed everyone but me in retaliation."

"Hmmm, I have killed a lot of people, but I do believe I remember the night in question. Do you remember what I told you that night?"

"That my father deserved to die because he stole from you. You also told me that a weak person was a dead person and to never let a person disrespect me," I replied.

Vincent nodded, and it was like a light bulb went off in my head.

"I apologize, ladies. I hope you two enjoy your baby shower, but I have something I need to do," I told Ari and Kenya.

"It's okay. We really need to plan a girl's day so we can catch up," Kenya replied.

I gave her a smile and stood. "Bye, everyone."

Everyone except Roman and his date told me goodbye. I put

my gun back in my tote and walked around the table to hug Mama before leaving.

Roman's date waited until I walked past her to mumble, "Bye, bitch," under her breath.

I turned around and walked back to the table. The woman's eyes got big when she saw me approach her. I picked up one of the gold knives from the table, stabbed her in the arm with it, and then turned back around to leave. The woman screamed loudly, but I kept walking. On my way out of the hotel, she was still screaming.

When I made it home, I took a shower and changed clothes. At exactly nine p.m., there was a knock on my door. I got off the living room couch and went to open the door. Greg walked through the door with a smile on his face. He was dressed to impress in a new black suit with a red tie and red dress shoes to complete his look. Ironically, he looked casket-sharp.

"Brittany, I must admit I was surprised to hear from you."

"Hmm, and I was surprised I called you. Come on," I told him and then walked up my stairs.

Greg followed me. I entered my bedroom and had a seat on the edge of my bed.

"Things got heated the day you left, and I admit I was wrong for the way I handled things. All I wanted to do, Brittany, was to love you and be there for you."

"Interesting. What do you want from me now after everything happened?"

"I still want us to be together. I ride by your house every day, but I didn't stop because I wasn't sure if you would want to see me."

Pathetic. Weak. Disrespectful.

"If you are serious about being with me, prove it. Take your clothes off and come show me how much you love me."

Greg took his time removing every item as if he thought getting naked in front of me would turn me on.

"Come here, baby. I want to take your clothes off," Greg said and held his hand out.

Yeah, no, that's not going to happen.

Instead of taking his hand, I stood and quickly removed the clothes I had on. Not even a minute later, we stood in front of each other naked. Greg took his time staring at every inch of my body.

"You like what you see?" I purred.

"Brittany, please give me a chance. Let me love you, baby."

"Put a condom on and come lay down on the bed. Let me ride you. I want to see your face when I cum all over your dick."

Greg's dick jumped while he reached down to pick his pants up off the floor and get a condom out. His hands shook while he tore the condom pack open and slid it down his dick. He took big steps toward me and my bed. I moved slightly to the right so he wouldn't touch me as he climbed on my bed.

"We been fucking for years, and you haven't sucked my dick once. When will you bless me with your mouth?"

Never in a million years.

"Maybe after this. I got a feeling this is going to be a night to remember."

Greg smiled as I climbed on top of his naked body. I could see precum leaking from the top of his dick in the condom. I reached down and jacked his dick a few times until Greg moaned and closed his eyes. My body lifted slightly, and I sat on top of his dick without inserting it in me. Back and forth, I rocked a few times, teasing him.

"Please, baby, it's been too long. I need to feel my dick inside you."

"That's the problem. You want something that doesn't fucking belong to you."

I slid a knife from under my pillow and plunged it into his chest over and over. Blood squirted everywhere, including on me, but I didn't stop. He was gasping for air and trying to reach out to stop me, but it was too late.

"Do you still want me now, Greg? HMMMMMM? DO YOU?"

Greg was still alive, but he had stopped fighting. His eyes had turned glossy, and his chest was barely moving up and down.

"I bet after this, you will understand that you shouldn't touch other people's property. I belong to one motherfucker, and his name is Roman BUCUR!"

The knife went in and out of his chest. I had to have stabbed him over fifty times before I plunged the knife into his chest one more time and left it there.

Slowly, I climbed off the bed and stared at Greg's body. I always wondered how I would feel if I lost my temper and killed someone. Now, I knew I would feel nothing.

Girl, what we about to do? Because orange is not my color, and we are not going to fucking prison!

I walked over to my nightstand and picked up my phone. My finger scrolled until I found the only person in the world I wanted to talk to. I hit call, prepared to hear the automated phone message again, but to my surprise, the phone rang.

Roman

"I need you," Brittany said when I answered the phone. There was something about her voice that made me stand up from the table.

"Baby, what's wrong? Talk to me."

"I killed him, Roman, and I need you."

Killed who? Did somebody touch obsesia mea (my obsession)?

"I'm on the way, baby," I replied.

The phone beeped two times, alerting me that she had hung up.

"What is wrong, brother?" Alexandur asked.

"I do not know, but I have to leave."

After the baby shower ended, we had to get movers to load all the gifts in two separate U-hauls and deliver the items to Kenya and Ari. We went to Ari and Constatin's house first to help them organize everything. Now, we were at Kenya and Alexandur's house. Everything had been put away, and I was just sitting at the kitchen table, listening to my brothers talk.

"We are going with you," Kofi stated.

I did not reply because I had already turned around and walked toward Alexandur's front door. In the background, I could hear all three of my brothers following me, but the only thing on my mind was making it to Brittany.

Outside of Alexandur's house, I hit the unlock button on my keyfob and got inside my car. My brothers opened my other car doors and climbed inside. As soon as I heard the last door close, I hit the button to start my car and pushed on the gas. Brittany didn't tell me if she was at home or not, but if she were anywhere else, she would have stated it.

Why would she be with another man at this time of night?

Jealousy mixed with fear had me pushing down on the gas pedal a little more. After Brittany stabbed Aniya in the arm, I warned her what would happen if anybody were to find out what Brittany did. At that moment, I decided it was time for her and I to have a discussion. When she left, Vincent told me that I would have been a fool to let a woman like Brittany go. The mafia world was really too damn small. Never would I have guessed that the man who killed Brittany's family was the leader of La Cosa Nostra, but it made sense. Vincent was the boss of bosses for a reason. The man was ruthless.

When I pulled into Brittany's yard, I frowned. The car parked next to Brittany's BMW belonged to her boss, Greg.

Is Greg the man she killed? If so, why?

I turned my car off and hopped out. When I reached Brittany's front door, I twisted the knob to see if it was unlocked, and it was.

"Baby," I called out as I entered her home, but there was no response.

I jogged through her hallway and up the stairs. Her bedroom door was open, and I sped up to see what the hell had happened. I entered her bedroom and froze.

"Oh, this motherfucker is crazy crazy," Kofi blurted out. I had forgotten my brothers were following me.

"Turn around," I demanded before walking farther into Brittany's bedroom.

Brittany stood in front of me naked, but there was so much

blood all over her body that it almost covered every inch of her skin. Greg was lying naked in her bed with a knife sticking out his chest.

She was not joking when she said she had killed him.

"Baby? What happened? How many times did you stab him?" I asked her while glancing around the room. There was too much blood to clean without leaving DNA evidence.

"I didn't count, but more than fifty and less than a hundred," she replied.

"Did she just say she stabbed that man over fifty times?" Kofi whispered to one of my other brothers.

Whoever he was whispering to did not respond.

"Did he hurt you, Brittany? Tell me what led up to this, so I know how much evidence I need to destroy."

"I called him and told him I missed him. He rushed over here as I expected. We came upstairs to my room, and I told him to get naked. He complied, and I followed right behind him. I lied and told him that I wanted to ride his dick. He lay in my bed, and I climbed on top of him. I told him he shouldn't touch other people's property, and I slid the knife from under my pillow and plunged it into his chest and stomach repeatedly. When I got tired, I climbed off him and called you."

"And they call me a monster. Roman done fell in love with a crazy bitch," Alexandur muttered.

"Whose property did he touch, Brittany?"

My heartbeat raced, and my palms got sweaty while I waited for her response.

"Your property, Roman. I belong to you, and you belong to me."

A smile crossed my face, and I reached out to grab Brittany's body. She snuggled into my chest, and we kissed each other passionately. Our tongues danced together, licking and sucking until we were both short of breath.

"I'm about to be sick. He's just kissing her like her body isn't covered in another man's blood. I got to stop hanging with y'all motherfuckers," Kofi stated.

I took my suit jacket off and put it on Brittany's body. Greg's body, phone, and car all needed to disappear. My baby did a decent job with her first murder, but we would have to work on her not making such a big mess.

"Take her in the bathroom and start her a shower. We need to discuss what all we need to do to make sure none of this points back to her," Constatin ordered.

"Come on, baby. Let's get you clean." I reached down to grab her hand and led her to her bedroom.

Brittany

Last night was a long night. After I murdered Greg and called Roman, he and his brothers came and took over. Roman bathed me and put fresh clothes on me. Kofi took Greg's phone so he could completely erase all contact between me and him that wasn't professional before destroying it. Constatin took Greg's car keys and drove his car to a chop shop. He told me by the end of the afternoon, Greg's car would be crushed, and the scraps sold for metal.

Alexandur helped Roman wrap Greg's body in my rug. They carried him outside and put him inside Roman's trunk. The last step was setting my house on fire. There was too much blood everywhere, so destroying my home was the best choice. We set the fire and left. Thirty minutes passed before I got a call from the fire department. I gave them Roman's address, and they came over to tell me what happened. As far as they knew, I went to a baby shower with my boyfriend and his family and then spent the rest of the night with them, helping organize gifts. Roman and I went to his home when we finished.

They didn't ask for proof, but we could provide several eyewitnesses if they asked in the future. When the fire department and police officers left, Roman and his brothers went into his basement and burned Greg's body and all the bloody clothes we were wearing. I fell asleep, waiting for Roman to finish in the basement and get into bed.

When I woke up not too long ago, I was still by myself in Roman's bed. His side of the bed looked slept in, but I was not a hundred percent positive if it really was or not. Roman came running to help me when I called him, and he treated me like he did before we broke up, but what did that mean? Was he ready to talk about what happened so we could move forward, or did he really not want to be with me anymore? If he didn't, I wouldn't give up. He told me that the best way to get rid of competition was to eliminate them, and I learned last night that killing was easy.

Roman's bedroom door opened, and he walked in carrying a tray of food. Confused, I frowned before sitting up in bed.

"Good morning, baby," Roman said before setting the tray of food on the nightstand.

"Good morning."

"I made you breakfast. You have lost weight, and I looked in your refrigerator last night, and there was barely any food in there."

"Will you stay in here to eat with me?"

He sat beside me on the bed and picked up the food tray. He brought a sliced piece of loaf bread with red sauce on it to my lips, and I took a bite. The taste of cooked vegetables and various herbs and spices coated my tongue. It was a flavor I wasn't used to, but it tasted delicious.

"What all did you cook?"

"What you just took a bite of was Zacusca. The omelet is stuffed with cheese, ham, and vegetables. The last item I cooked is Slanina. It's an extremely expensive meat pork belly that I grew up eating regularly."

I reached over on the tray, picked up a piece of Slanina, and brought it to Roman's lips. He opened his mouth and ate it. We took turns feeding each other until the breakfast plate was empty.

"What do we do now?" I asked.

"We talk. I am going to clean this dish. I will be right back," he replied.

Roman took the dish back out of his room, and I waited patiently for him to return. It didn't take him long to return. He sat back down on the bed beside me.

"What do you want, Brittany?"

"I want us to get back together and never break up again. Do you want the same thing, Roman?"

"Yes, I love you with all my heart. I want a marriage and kids one day with you and only you."

Marriage maybe. Kids, probably not.

"If marrying you will make you happy, I might do it, but you can't take my ring from me. It is mine."

"If that is the ring you want to keep, no problem. How do you feel about me?"

"It's hard to express how I feel about you because I am not familiar with the feelings swirling around inside me. What I do know is that I belong to you. I only want you. You are mine and will be mine until the day I die."

Roman smiled. I guessed he liked my answer.

"That is good enough for me, Brittany. The next time a man gets close to you, kill him or let me kill him, but do not let him touch you."

"The same rule applies to you. A woman approaches you, you better tell her that your woman is crazy, and she will kill they ass."

Roman laughed before reaching out to pull my face to his. We kissed each other deeply while he squeezed my neck. He didn't squeeze tight enough to cut off my access to oxygen, but it was enough to make me lightheaded. My pussy was leaking, and I could feel my panties getting wet. I broke the kiss and stood up to remove my clothes. Roman watched me get naked before he stood and took all his clothes off. As soon as he stepped out of his briefs, I was on him like white on rice. The last time we fucked was over three weeks ago, and I needed his dick inside me now.

"Have you been a good girl, Brittany, or have you been naughty?"

"Naughty, Roman. I've been naughty."

Roman smirked at me before grabbing a handful of my hair and tossing me on the bed. He climbed on top of me and squeezed my breasts. I moaned, my body already shaking lightly in anticipation. Roman placed kisses all down my body until he reached my pussy. He spread my legs wide and buried his face between my legs. His hands went under my hips, and he lifted them slightly off the bed. More of my pussy secretions leaked out of me and onto his face. I thought he was about to eat my pussy until I felt his thick tongue slide into my ass.

"Fuck!" I screamed.

In and out, he moved his tongue in my ass. The feeling of ecstasy hit my body, and I grabbed the sheets. My legs started to tremble, and I could feel my orgasm building. Roman stopped tongue fucking my ass, and I whined.

"Roman, I was about to cum!"

"Naughty girls have to get punished first, baby."

He moved from between my legs and flipped me over on my back. My whole body lay flat on the bed.

"Use your words, baby. Tell me what I want to hear."

Part of me wanted to be defiant and tell him no, but my desire to cum was stronger.

"I belong to you," I whispered.

"Good girl."

Roman smacked me on my ass cheeks before spreading them wide. He spat on my asshole before I felt his dick pushing slowly inside it. Pain hit my body, and I gasped for air.

Roman slowly pushed his dick into my ass, inch by inch, until his dick was fully inside me. He did not move at first. Instead, he lay his body down flat against mine.

"Talk to me, baby. Tell me how it feels to have your ass stuffed with my nine-inch-long dick," he whispered in my ear.

A shiver went through my body, and I could feel my pussy walls tightening.

"It hurts so good. Roman, please fuck me," I begged.

Roman began to move his hips back and forth. His thrusts were deep, and my asshole felt like it was about to split into two pieces.

"Fuck. I am so proud of you, baby," he praised me. Roman leaned off me and pulled me up on my knees before increasing the speed of his thrusts.

"Yessssss!" I moaned loudly. There was something about receiving pain and pleasure at the same time that made my body feel alive.

"Do not cum yet, Brittany. You haven't earned the right."

Oh, my god! What the fuck?

"Please, baby. I will be your good girl. Pleaseeeeeeeeee," I cried.

My orgasm was right there, and I was trying everything I could to stop myself from erupting.

Roman stopped fucking me and pulled his dick out of my ass. I heard him get off the bed and dig into the drawer on his nightstand. A naughty girl would have turned around to see what he was doing, but only good girls got to cum, so I kept my body in the same position without moving.

Roman climbed back on the bed.

"Turn around and lay flat, baby."

I did as he asked and waited to see what he was about to do next.

Roman climbed between my legs and put both of my legs on his shoulders. He slid his dick inside my pussy and began to fuck me. My toes curled, and I felt pleasure build in my body again.

"I love you, Brittany. My life is not complete without you in it."

My body started to shake, and tears formed in my eyes.

"Can I cum on your dick?"

Roman groaned, and I heard a flickering sound.

"You can cum if you mark my heart like I marked yours."

Roman handed me the lighter and fucked me harder. My hands trembled, but I flicked the lighter on and moved it to his chest. The orange and blue flames danced against the tattoo he had on his chest. I looked up at him, and he nodded. My hand moved the lighter closer to him, and I watched as the flame burned his skin. Roman threw his head back and groaned.

"Good girl. Baby, hold it steady."

The smell of burning flesh mixed with the smell of sex was intoxicating. My orgasm smacked into my body out of nowhere, and I screamed. The lighter dropped out of my hand while my body jerked uncontrollably.

"AHHHHHHHHHH!" Roman screamed. He released so much nut inside my pussy that I could feel it leaking out of me and onto the sheets.

Roman collapsed on top of me. He wrapped his arms around my body tight. We stayed like that until Roman got up. He scooped me up and carried me to the shower.

Roman

"Are you ready, baby?" I asked Brittany.

Brittany and I had been living together for almost three months. The day after we burned her house down and made love, I took her shopping to replace all the items she lost. After we finished clothes shopping, we went house shopping because I wanted her to feel comfortable in our home. Phoebe had her own room with everything a cat could want. I added Brittany's name to the deed to show her that what was once mine is now ours.

"Yes, here I come."

A few minutes later, Brittany walked down the stairs toward me. The weather outside was beginning to heat up. Brittany had on a pair of black shorts with a black and white t-shirt and some Yeezy crops. When Brittany stepped off the bottom step, I reached out to grab her hand and let her out of our front door. The tattoo shop that we were going to would be closed over the next four hours while we got our tattoos done. The man who would do them is the same one who did all of my and my family's tattoos.

I opened the passenger side door for Brittany and helped her get inside my Bugatti before I walked around and opened the door to climb inside. After Buckling my seatbelt, I leaned over to place a kiss on Brittany's forehead before I hit the start button on my car. A few minutes later, we pulled out of our driveway.

"You know I love you, right?" I asked her.

"Yes, and you know I belong to you, right?" she replied.

I smiled before taking one hand off the steering wheel to join our hands together while using the other one to continue driving. Brittany did not have to tell me she loved me because I knew she did, even if she wasn't able to express the emotion. She showed me every day how much I meant to her, and I was happy she came into my life. When you truly love someone, you accept them as they are. Brittany might have been a sociopath, but she was my sociopath. In the same way, I was a psychopath, but I was her psychopath. It might sound crazy to people on the outside looking in, but what we had worked for us, and that was all that mattered.

The drive to the tattoo shop only took about thirty minutes. I pulled into the parking lot and parked my car before getting out to open the door for Brittany. We joined hands and walked together into the tattoo shop.

"What's good?" the tattoo artist said.

"Hey, are you ready for us?"

"Yeah, come on to the back. How many tattoos are y'all getting today.?"

"We are getting a total of three tattoos. The first one will be a yellow eagle, and I want it on Brittany's neck. The next one will be a tattoo that says 'Property of Brittany,' and I want it in bold black letters going across my stomach."

Brittany wanted me to get it on my chest, but I had so many tattoos on my chest that we would have had to find a small spot, and that was not going to work for me. I wanted the world to know who I belonged to, so we agreed to get it across my stomach, where I did not have any tattoos.

"The last tattoo will say 'Property of Roman,' and she will be getting it on her right ass cheek."

It took a lot of pussy eating and dick slinging for me to finally get her to agree to get this tattoo on her ass. When it was time for us to get our tattoos done, I saw the look on the man's face when he saw the burn marks all over Brittany's and my bodies. Wisely, he decided to keep his mouth shut and worry about himself and the life he enjoyed living. As I stated before, everybody on the outside looking in would not understand me and Brittany's love, but it was nobody's business but our own.

Epilogue
The Mind

Five years later

"Dad, can I go over to Uncle Roman and Auntie Brittany's house?" my son Mischief asked me.

I do not know what in the world my brother and his wife do to my son, but every day after school, he has been asking to go over there. It had been going on for almost three months, and something just did not feel right about it. Roman and Brittany were the only two who did not have kids. When I asked Roman if they ever would, he said it was up to his wife, but she did not want any right now. Brittany was good to my brother, and she made him happy, so I was okay with whatever they decided.

So, why did my son always want to go over to their house and spend time with them? He had more toys here. He owned every game system you could think of, and every weekend, I took him somewhere to have a father-and-son fun day.

"Dad," my son called my name out again to get my attention.

My wife came waddling into the room, and Mischief temporarily forgot about me to run to her. He placed a kiss on her swollen belly before hugging her tight. Ari made me wait until she graduated college with her master's degree in nursing and opened a clinic with Brittany before I could get her pregnant again. We were having a girl and naming her Mystic. My wife waited until my son let her go to come over and give me a kiss.

"Regina Mea (my queen), we are having a baby in a month. When are you planning to stop working?"

She rolled her eyes and shot me a bird. Mischief burst out laughing. My wife was still as beautiful and feisty as she was when I met her at my brother's wedding. It did not matter what was going on with the mafia or the wine company. As long as my wife and kids were safe and happy, I knew I could face anything that came my way.

"Ma, I asked Dad if I could go over to Uncle Roman and Auntie Brittany's house, and he isn't letting me."

"Mischief, stop lying. That's why I am hesitating to let you go over there. Who knows what they are over there teaching you?"

"Uncle Roman takes me hunting to kill real animals, and Aunty Brittany teaches me how to manipulate people by being charming."

Ari began to laugh as if what our son said was funny.

"How about we go outside and play basketball?"

My son looked at me with a frown on his face.

"Let's make a deal, Dad. If I get an A on all my tests this week, I can spend the weekend with Uncle Roman and Auntie Brittany."

I thought about what he said. Mischief had been in private school since the age of two, and he always excelled in his grades, but lately, he had been bringing home a lot of Bs.

"You have a deal, son."

Mischief ran to me and gave me a hug before running up the stairs to play in his room. My wife waited until he was all the way up the stairs before shaking her head at me.

"What I do?" I asked her.

"You just let a four-year-old play you," she replied.

Play me? How??

"Explain. I am lost."

"Constatin, your son has had the highest grade in his class for two years, and now that he is hanging with his uncle and auntie, his grades are slipping. What does that mean?"

"It means he needs to stay home more and study."

"No, my dear, clueless husband. It means your son is purposely missing questions on his tests so he can have leverage to use to get his way."

"No way. He is only four. He would not do something like that."

"If our son comes home with all As and you do not see him studying, then you, sir, have been played. When you realize I'm right, I want a new Hermes purse."

Ari wobbled over to give me another kiss before heading toward the kitchen.

I watched my son all week, and he did not open one book to study, but he brought home straight As. On Friday, I sent my wife a million dollars and told her it was for another Hermes purse.

The Monster

Five years later

"Sotie mea (my wife), you already own eleven Hooters in Georgia. Why do you need to own more?"

"Because I want more," she replied.

Normally, Kenya got whatever Kenya wanted, but the more Hooters my wife took over, the more time she spent away from home.

"No, my answer is permanent, and it will not change."

"If you buy me another Hooters, I will push another one of your big head ass babies out of my vagina."

Fuck. She knows I want one more child. Artemis just turned four, and the twins, Apollo and Aphrodite, are two. Now would be the perfect time to have our last child.

"If you are lying, I will put you in time out for a whole week."

"Baby, if you buy me another Hooters, you can dig inside me and pull the Mirena out yourself."

"Will it hurt you?"

"No, I heard a girl at work tell her friend that her man removed hers, and she got pregnant a month later."

"Hmmmm, if it does not work, you will go to the doctor to make sure you are off birth control?"

"Yes, Alexandur. Are you going to buy it for me?"

"Of course. We have an hour until nap time is over. I want you naked on the bed with your legs spread wide. It is time for Dr. Monster to perform a procedure."

My wife laughed before running up the stairs to do as I asked. A few minutes later, I got up and walked up the stairs behind her. The nursery was in the room right next to ours. I peeked my head inside to check on my kids. They were all asleep without a care in the world. Six years ago, if somebody had told me I would fall in love and have a house full of kids, I would have shot them. Now, I know that everyone deserves real love, including monsters.

The Mystery

"Mischief texted me. He is spending the weekend with us."

Obsesia Mea (my obsession) was good with all the kids in my family, but Mischief loved spending time with her the most.

"You win, Roman. We can have a child."

"Huh?"

Did she say what I think she just said?

"Roman, do you really believe that you have been manipulating me all these years without me knowing it? Whenever you want me to do something that you know there's a chance I won't do, you manipulate me. When you wanted us to get married, and I really didn't see the point in it because either way, you belong to me, and I belong to you, and that wasn't gonna change, you had your mother tell me how lonely she was since your father's death, and how she needed something to do to keep her busy, or she would fall into a depression. And then you mention to me how the only time she is happy is when she's planning a major event for the family, like a wedding or baby shower, and you hope something comes up soon because depression kills, and you didn't want to lose your mother.

"So, I went along with it and told you that if you proposed, I wouldn't turn you down. Of course, not even a week later, you got down on one knee. Now, you are manipulating me into having a child. Every time Mischief comes over, you tell me to teach him things that you know I enjoy teaching, like how to be manipulative or how to hurt others, to show me that we can still be ourselves and raise a baby. So, you win, husband, I already made an appointment to get off birth control on Monday."

I turned the temperature on the stove to low and turned around to scoop my wife up in my arms. She was right. I had been manipulating her, but the fact that she has known and gone along with it all this time is why I love her so much. My wife was my property, and I was hers.

The End

Author's Note

First, I want to thank you all for supporting me. There are no words to describe how grateful I am. I am an avid reader. Any book that has romance in it, I will read it, but dark romance has always held a special place in my heart. When I decided to switch lanes and give it a try, I was terrified. I was not sure how my readers would take it. To my surprise and delight, my first dark romance series has been a success. I have you all to thank for that success. Dark romance may be a new lane for me, but it is a lane I plan to stay in for a while. To celebrate the success of The Devil Wears Baccarat series, I am selling book boxes. A pre-order link to purchase them will be available on my Facebook page on October 25th at 8:00 a.m. Central Standard Time. I will only be selling a limited amount, and the sale will only last over the weekend unless that amount is reached before then. Pictures will be posted when it gets closer to the 25th, but each box will have all three books, a customized hoodie, a tumbler, and smaller items such as a magnet and stickers. Below are my social media handles, where I post all updated information.

Facebook: Author Jatoria Crews
TikTok: Author Jatoria C

Instagram: Author Jatoria C

A new book will be dropping in December. Thank you. Thank you. Thank you.

Also by Jatoria C.

The Devil Wears Baccarat 2
The Devil Wears Baccarat
Obsessed With A Plus Size Barbie 3
Obsessed With A Plus Size Barbie 2
Obsessed With A Plus Size Barbie
Alexa, Play I Need A Rich Thug Husband 2
Alexa, Play I Need A Rich Thug Husband